TOM

and

G.E.R.I.

C. A. KNUTSEN

Acknowledgements

I would like to thank Judy Knutsen, Kenneth Kussmann, and Russell Beard for their thorough reading of a proof copy and their feedback.

caknutsen.com

ISBN - 13: 978-1-7330003-3-8

Cover Art by Christian Bentulan

for

Bob

1.

It took me all day to get that car out. Well, it wasn't a car. That's just what I thought it might be when I spotted part of it jutting out from decades of forest undergrowth, and moss, inside a mound of blackberry bushes. So the name stuck. I still don't have a better one.

I finally had managed to buy the Simpson place. Old man Simpson had been in his eighties when he died. He'd been living in the family home by himself for a long time. He had a stern, angry manner that drove Mrs. Simpson and their only child, Rachel, away. He hadn't done much to keep the place up. As shabby as the house and the rest of it was, Mrs. Simpson, who had inherited it, wouldn't sell it. When she died, Rachel accepted my offer, wanting nothing more to do with the place.

I had been interested in the land, one hundred acres in all, since I was a young boy growing up near there. Except for where the house and barn were and a few acres of fields around them, it was covered with evergreen trees, mostly fir. The land rose up into the foothills of the North Cascade Range.

As a boy I got excited just thinking about what could be in that forest and up in those hills. I tried exploring it several times back then. Simpson would see me, and chase me away, yelling at me in his hate-filled voice.

So it happened that I didn't get to see much of the land. The mystery of it was at the center of my desire to have it as my own. On Sunday night, after I bought the place I came back to the small town of Tipton, my hometown, and rented a room at Mrs. Jorgensen's Boarding House. The next morning I drove out to finally do the exploring I had always wanted to do. Simpson's land was at the end of Tyler Road, a few miles past the house where I grew up.

The house and barn were all gray and weathered looking, but I hadn't bought it for the buildings. Through the windows of the house I saw nothing of interest, so I went to the barn. With everything else in such disrepair I was surprised to find a large tractor in the barn that, except for a thick coating of dust, looked brand new. That was interesting, but I was there for the forest.

When I got to the edge of the forest, I found it hard to believe I was finally getting a chance to walk beneath those trees and learn their secrets. I knew I'd be exploring all day, so I had brought a pack with food and water and had worn sturdy clothes and boots. As it turned out it was a good thing that I had. I saw that it was going to be a challenging trek. It wasn't a dense forest. There was plenty of light getting to the ground supporting salal and other undergrowth. Which made walking more difficult. I looked around for a path.

What I found might have been a road fifty or more years ago. There were bushes in the road, but the ground was level, which helped. As I walked along, my eyes examined every tree and bush seeking out the unusual.

There was a quietness in the forest. I could see my breath in the cold October morning air. I could hear my breathing and the noise I made as I pushed my way through the bushes but little else. As the road narrowed it was difficult to sense direction. The trees and brush looked the same everywhere. I had brought a compass and checked it occasionally to keep oriented.

After about an hour into the forest I was surprised by an open space appearing before me. It was roughly circular and about thirty feet across. It was covered with ferns. It was obvious that no one had trod across the clearing for a long time. In the center of the clearing there was a mound of blackberry brambles that intrigued me.

Blackberry stalks usually needed something to climb on to build a mound that high. The mound was about twelve feet long, and eight feet wide and tall. If there was something there it was probably large. I wanted to find out what it was.

As I got closer, I could see that the berries had dried and shriveled on the vines. As I looked into the complex weaving of stalks, I saw was a mound of dried berry stalks and leaves, a smattering of bushes in the mix, and a generous covering of moss. I thought that perhaps that was all there was. The bushes could have been what the stalks climbed up and over. I was about to give up when I saw a part of some sort of metal-like surface jutting out of the bushes inside the mound.

A road had led into the forest, so the surface I saw was likely part of a derelict truck or car. By the apparent size and height, I settled on a car. So, the bushes and berry stalks had captured an old car. I was disappointed. I was hoping for something more mysterious.

So far in my day's exploration I had discovered an unusual clearing in the forest. In the clearing was an old car covered by brambles. I had a decision to make. Should I go farther into the forest on this first expedition, or was digging into this unexpected mound to be my focus for the day?

If I stayed here to learn more about the car and what might be in it, I would have to clear away the brambles. I wasn't equipped for that. I might find what I needed in my newly acquired barn, but even if I did, carrying the necessary tools into the woods this far would be a chore. Then I thought about the tractor. If I could find the tools, and if I could get the tractor started, I could use the tractor to carry the tools at least most of the way. That sounded like an adventure. So after a brief lunch, I walked back to the barn to see what I could find.

I opened the large double barn doors all the way to let in as much light and fresh air as I could. I rummaged around the interior and found a mattock, a shovel, a long-handled branch pruner and smaller pruners. I cleaned the dust off everything and found some oil for the pruners. I also found a coil of rope and a pair of serviceable leather gloves. I thought the rope might come in handy. I knew the gloves would.

I put the tools in a bin behind the cab of the tractor. The tractor was a large, green, John Deere, multi-purpose farm vehicle. I climbed up into the spacious cab. I was surprised but pleased that the key was in the ignition. Turning the key, the engine came alive on the first try, another surprise. I drove around the yard to get used to the gears and then set out for the forest.

I started off at reasonable speed but quickly had to slow down when the tractor began bouncing up and down. I looked down into the overgrown field. There were small irrigation channels that still held their shape even after years of not being used. Looking around I found a smoother path.

The going was easier when I got on the old road leading into the forest. The tractor's wheels were so large that the chassis was higher than the bushes in the road, and the wheelbase was narrow enough that the tractor was able to pass even when I got to the place where the forest encroached on the road.

Parking the tractor at the edge of the clearing, I put on the gloves and took the tools over to the bramble mound and began working. I only had to clear away a quarter of the blackberry mound to get access to the bushes surrounding the car. I cut the blackberry vines and the other bushes at the ground level. When

I moved them out of the way, I learned that I had found something quite different from a rusted out old car.

Moss was covering the decaying vegetation on the surface. Brushing that away I saw that there was no rust or moss on the metal. From the age of the mound this whatever-it-was had to have been here a long time. So why was there no rust? The mystery drove me to quickly clear away the rest of the vegetation so I could see what the whole thing looked like.

It wasn't a car. First off there were no wheels, nor any place for them that I could see. I couldn't see all of it because its nose was down into the dirt as if it had hit the dirt with some force. It was ten feet long and seven feet wide. It was about seven feet tall and flat at the back and on the sides. It sloped down at the front. It was a dark-green, bronze color. The surface was untouched by time or weather. There were a few pock marks near the front and what looked like a scorch along one side.

I needed to get all of it above ground on a level surface if I was going to learn more about it. To do that I would need to shovel the ground away from where its nose was buried. I cleared enough of the rest of the brush away to give me room to work. As it turned out that meant that all of the blackberry vines had to go. So I cut them all and pitched them off to the side. Once that was done, I started digging. The ground was hard as a brick around where the nose had dug in. The mattock broke it up, but it took a while. The rest of the ground was soft forest floor with no roots or major rocks to contend with.

It took me nearly an hour to expose the entire vehicle. I was right in my first assessment. There were no wheels. The bottom looked to be flat, but I couldn't be sure until I raised it up high enough to see it. I had exposed enough of it that I was sure I could get the rope around it and maybe use the tractor to drag it out of the hole it had made in the ground.

I went back to the tractor. I didn't want to tear up the floor of this clearing that had gone untouched for so many years, but if I was going to get the thing out of its hole and out of the clearing I could see no other way. I was about to go inside the cab to get things started when I happened to look over my shoulder and stopped in my tracks.

I turned completely around to make sure of what I was seeing. I needn't have worried about getting the vehicle out of the hole. It had done that by itself. It was floating about a foot above the surface of the hole it had come out of. There was no noise. There were no lights blinking. It was simply floating. This thing definitely did not come out of the Buick showroom downtown.

I could see its entire shape. It was made up of straight lines all around, and it did slope down to about three feet high at what I thought of as the front. I could stand where I was all day, or I could step forward for a closer look. I walked to within a few feet of where it was floating. I could hear a quiet hum coming from it.

I stepped closer and there was no reaction from it. Trying not to fall in the hole it had just come out of, I came up next to it. I carefully reached out and touched it. It was cool to the touch, slightly colder than the late afternoon air. It seemed to move slightly. Emboldened, I gently pushed it, and it moved in response. Maybe I wouldn't have to disturb the clearing. Maybe I could push it or pull it where I wanted to take it.

So where did I want to take it? The barn was the obvious answer. It had been a long day and being October it was getting dark already. That would help. My newly acquired farm was at the end of the road. The forest I was in was even farther away from the road, behind the house and barn. Still, it was possible that someone might be looking in my direction. It would be better if there was less light as I towed it to the barn which was what I set out to do.

I pushed the thing away from the hole and turned it around so that what I thought was its back was pointed toward the tractor. I got in front of it and pushed it over directly behind the tractor. The thing seemed to go wherever I pushed or pulled it with little effort. I just needed to rope it so that it followed the tractor. I'm sure someone could have improved on my harness, but I knew it would work.

Perhaps I was already getting paranoid about my new find, but I felt compelled to cover the hole it had come from. When I had shoveled the dirt back in the hole and piled all the cut brush over it, I felt better.

Starting the tractor I began slowly going back the way I had come earlier. The thing I was towing rose and fell as it floated over the various heights of the bushes. By the time I got to the barn it was very dark. The clouds had rolled in and there was no moon. I pulled the tractor and its cargo into the barn. I exited the barn, closed the doors, and locked it with a padlock. I drove back to town. I was more tired than hungry. I was exhausted by the work and the experience of finding a floating vehicle. I just went to bed and tried to sleep.

2.

That was yesterday.

This morning I was having breakfast at Mel's Diner. I was sipping my second cup of coffee trying to avoid thinking about what was in my barn and what I was going to do about it. So far I had not come up with anything. I needed a distraction.

I thought about how I had met Eleanor Jorgensen when I checked into Mrs. Jorgensen's Boarding House. The Boarding House had been a fixture of Tipton since before I was born. Eleanor had helped her mom as she was growing up, and when her mother died, she took over running it. Eleanor could have changed the name to Miss Jorgensen's Boarding House, but she said that just didn't seem right.

I knew Eleanor from school. She was a couple of grades behind me. I always liked her. She had a smile that seemed to warm my heart. Eleanor had been about my height, with broad shoulders and a narrow waist. She had been taller than the other girls and some of the boys had teased her about it. The teasing stopped when she broke Jimmy Saunders' nose.

Jimmy's dad ran the Tipton Lumber Mill back then. Jimmy acted as if he was better than everyone else since most of our fathers worked for his dad.

One school night a number of the kids had gathered around the Tasty Freeze talking and playing around. Jimmy had been drinking beer and was full of himself. He had been trying to get Eleanor to go out with him. She was one of the best-looking girls in school, and Jimmy wanted her to be his girlfriend. He thought she should be grateful for his attention and was getting angry that she didn't see it that way.

Jimmy walked up to Eleanor and tried to put his arm around her. She pushed him away. He came back, tried again, and this time his hand touched one of her breasts. Eleanor stepped back and punched him in the face. Jimmy stumbled back, tripped, hit his head on the pavement, and was out cold.

The next day Eleanor came into school with a support bandage wrapped around her sprained wrist. Jimmy came in with a bandage over his broken nose.

After that Eleanor became more popular with the girls. The boys were a bit intimidated. For a while the boys called her One-Punch-Jorgensen, but that stopped quickly. Eleanor didn't like it. Neither did her older brother, Billy, who was bigger than most of the boys. Jimmy Saunders faded into the background, drank more, and eventually killed himself when he drove his car into a tree along Millers Road.

I always thought fondly of Eleanor and was a little shy around her when I checked into the Boarding House. Her smile still warmed me, but now as a woman her smile also made me a little wobbly in the knees. Her lustrous blonde hair came down to her neck and surrounded her face which had only become lovelier. She was still my height, and her figure had, well, improved with age.

She was so beautiful that I wondered why it was she had never married. I certainly wasn't going to ask her. She was less reserved and asked me why I never had. I told her I hadn't found the right person. She paused to think about what I'd said, and then nodded as if she knew what I meant.

The Boarding House was an anomaly in today's world. There are a lot of bed-and-breakfast places where people stayed a night or two. The Boarding House was more like a bed-and-dinner place where people stayed for longer periods and shared an evening meal with the owner and other boarders. Breakfast was provided, but you could also get breakfast and lunch at Mel's Diner.

During the time I had lived in Tipton, Mel's Diner was run by Melinda Archer. Her son Melvin took over when she retired. Melvin was about five-foot ten, had a slender build with light brown, wispy hair. He was wearing a linen apron with "Eat at Mel's Diner" printed on it over a clean white tee shirt and light-colored cotton pants, an outfit that seemed right for the owner and main cook at a diner.

When I came in earlier, Melvin had looked at me as if he were trying to place who I was. It was obvious that he thought he knew me but wasn't sure. Apparently, his curiosity overpowered his fear of embarrassment, as he was coming my way with the coffee pot even though my cup was still nearly full.

"Aren't you…?" Mel asked, as he came up to the table.

"Yes. Tom Williams. Good to see you Mel."

"Tom Williams! Of course! Where ya been, Tom? You left after your folks died, and we all wondered what happened to you."

I was going to get that question a lot. *Died,* isn't the word I used to describe what happened to my parents. They were *killed* by a drunk driver when they were driving home on Highway 2 in the summer after I graduated from high school.

Afterward I was in a fog. People would come up and tell me how sorry they were. I barely acknowledged them. I might have gone completely off the rails if it hadn't been for Frank Wilkins, our family's attorney. I was walking down Main Street unconscious of the world around me. Frank saw me, came out of his office, grabbed me by the arm, pulled me into his office, and sat me down.

Frank didn't coddle me saying how sorry he was. He shouted my name until he broke me out of my semi-conscious state and got my attention. Once he did, he told me that I needed to get back among the living and make something of myself. Then he helped me to get started.

I wasn't in any shape to go to college, though I had received many letters from colleges inviting me to apply. I was, and still am, a pretty smart boy, but in the mental state I was in I would have made a mess of my freshman year no matter what college I went to. Frank and I talked several times after that first wake-up chat. I decided to go into the Air Force. Frank wasn't pleased with my decision, neither was I really, but he stood by me.

With my help, he gathered everything in my parents' estate, and put it into a trust which would give me a monthly allotment to help support myself until I got out of the Air Force. After that the entire trust would revert to me. He managed the sale of my family home. When it sold after I left, he added the proceeds to the trust. I sincerely appreciated what Frank did for me then, and I've kept in touch with him since. It was through Frank that I made the purchase of the Simpson place.

"I joined the Air Force," I told Mel. "When my four years were up, I worked for a small tech company."

"It must be, what, fifteen years since you left town?" Mel asked, thinking out loud.

"That's about right."

"I heard you bought the old Simpson place out on Tyler road. That right?"

"Yes."

"Why?"

Small town people are nosy. They expect you to tell them everything so they can tell others. I knew this. I grew up in Tipton. I could tell Mel a little about why I bought it, but I didn't want the conversation to go on long, or drift into what I had found out there.

"I always wanted to see what was up in those woods. When I was a boy, Simpson chased me away, so I never had the chance."

"Heck, now that he's dead, you could have just gone out there, and looked around as much as you wanted. You didn't need to buy it," Mel asserted.

"Yes, I did."

As much as Tipton people wanted to know everything, I wasn't the type to explain myself. So I didn't. Mel changed the subject.

"Now that you own the place, are you planning to stay around?"

"I'm not that far along in my thinking, Mel. Could be, but I'm not sure."

I was saved from additional questions by another of Mel's customers wanting coffee. When he went to serve the coffee I got up, paid the cashier, and left. I didn't want to talk anymore. Also, I knew I shouldn't put off getting back to whatever it was that I had put in my barn yesterday. Who knows what the thing would be doing now that it was apparently active enough to float?

3.

People in town will continue to call my new acquisition "the Old Simpson place," but I won't. It's mine, and like his daughter Rachael the less I thought about Simpson the better. On the way out to my place this morning, I thought about the conversation with Mel. There was more to my experience since I left Tipton, than what I had told him.

It was true as far as it went. I did join and leave the Air Force and did work for a small electronics company. The rest was more interesting. Toward the end of my time in the Air Force, I had the opportunity to work on some experimental technology that the government had purchased from the two men who had developed it.

I met the developers when they installed the technology at Edwards Air Force Base. When they learned I was leaving the Air Force they asked me to join their organization, which had moved into a small warehouse nearby. They had expanded their operation to include a few more people and had continued to develop innovative technology. They couldn't pay me in cash, but they were impressed with my work and paid me in stock. I had plenty of money from the trust Frank set up so that was fine with me.

A few years later, that little start-up was purchased for an enormous amount of cash and stock options. I ended up with a tidy sum and gave Rachael a more than fair price for her land. My net worth, if known, would set me apart from Tipton society and I didn't want that to happen. So what I told Mel about my past would be the answer I would give every time a Tiptonite asked the question.

Twenty minutes after leaving Mel's I drove up to the barn. I heard some banging in the barn and noticed that it smelled like something had burned recently. When I went in and looked where my discovery from the day before had been tied up, I found out why. Somehow, it had freed itself by neatly slicing through the rope with something extremely hot.

I looked around to see if it was still in the barn and heard some banging from the loft. Stepping back I saw it bumping itself into the hayloft door apparently trying to get out. Perhaps it couldn't break out, or perhaps it didn't want to damage my barn. Either way it had to stop what it was doing.

I had no reason to believe it would understand what I said, but I tried talking to it anyway.

"Hey! Stop that!"

It turned around and pointed itself at me. I swear it looked like it was listening to me. That gave me the willies.

"If you want out, come down here and I'll let you out the front door."

It came down and hovered by me. Now I knew it understood me at some level, which made me more curious than concerned.

"I'll let you out, but before you leave, I need to tell you a few things. If you fly out of here you will be seen by people, and likely detected by the Air Force. They will send a fighter jet to look you over. If you run, they will chase you to find out what you are. If you look dangerous, they will fire a missile at you. If you don't, they will try to force you to land, and send someone out to capture you. If that happens, they will spend years working you over trying to figure out how you function. You'll be their prisoner and you won't be able to leave."

That was a lot to say to a dark-green, bronze colored, blocky vehicle which might not understand any of it. Still, it hovered in front of me and looked like it was listening to my every word. I decided to go a bit further.

"So if you leave you will need to be invisible."

Then I got a surprise. It disappeared.

"You still there?" I asked.

I thought I might be talking to myself for a moment. Then it reappeared hovering in the same place. Well, in for a penny....

"Okay. So those on the ground might not be able to see you with their eyes. The government has satellites that can detect you even if you can't be seen. They can see you if you are made of a metal that can be detected by their systems. Even if you aren't made of metal, they can capture thermal images."

It went around me toward the door. If it understood what I was saying apparently it thought it was safe from detection. Now I began to think about my offer to let it go. I was getting very curious and would like to learn more about my visitor. Still, whatever it was, I had no right to keep it.

"Okay, looks like you feel you'll be safe out there. Before you leave, you should give some thought about where you will go. If you have flight capability to get back to where you came from that's fine, but I suggest you leave our atmosphere quickly. If you plan to stay on Earth, but aren't sure where, you're welcome to stay here while you think it over."

I felt like I was a parent sending my kid off to their first day at school. I went to the barn doors and opened them completely. I turned around and stepped aside. It disappeared from sight, but I felt the air move as it sped by me on its way toward whatever destination it had in mind.

I had mixed emotions about it leaving. The thing was obviously not from around here, meaning from Earth. That was fascinating. On the other hand, it would probably bring me more trouble than I wanted. If word got around that I had a strange flying (and who knows what other kind of) machine, more people would be coming to my farm than the one out in mid-America where they made a baseball field out of a patch of corn. The government would find out and take it away to that dark future I had just described for it.

Nope. Overall, it's best that I let it go. I have the forest before me that I have always wanted. That was enough for me before I discovered the thing in the clearing, and it was still enough.

Unfortunately that would have to wait. It was time to go into the house and clean it out. I closed the barn doors. Just as I was about to put the lock on the hasp, I changed my mind. I opened the doors all the way and walked off toward the house. Well, you never know.

I went to my SUV to get some large plastic bags and a box of vinyl gloves I had purchased. Then I went over to the house and up the step to the front door. I didn't relish going in. The place still felt like that ornery old man that lived here for so many years.

I knew there was only one way to rid the place of his lingering presence. I had to open all the doors and windows, let fresh air flow through the house, and throw out everything that was in it. I'd try to find a way to pass on anything that was useful, but I wouldn't work too hard at it.

I put on my first pair of gloves and opened the door. I went around the first floor opening all the windows that would open, and then opened the back door. I went upstairs and opened the few windows that would open. It was forty-five degrees outside so the house cooled down quickly as it was airing out. I only glanced at things as I ran around. I didn't want to be distracted from my primary objective. It felt better already.

Now for the detailed work. I would have called Rachael to ask if she wanted any of this, but I thought I knew what her answer would be. The living room had a sofa and a few overstuffed chairs. I would get rid of the furniture later. For now they would be the places on and around which I would be piling the stuff that was on its way out the door.

I started with the closets downstairs. Coats and clothes went on the sofa. Junk went in the corner by the old TV. Junk was what I called everything that wasn't clothes. I used the large black plastic bags for trash. There was a china hutch in one corner. I left the items on display in the upper part where they were for now. I went through the drawers of the lower part. I found some tablecloths and napkins that looked like they had been left in place since Mrs. Simpson had left. They stayed where they were.

The top drawer contained old letters, some photos and other papers. I checked to see if there was anything valuable, or official that Rachael might need even if she didn't want it. I didn't find anything. I went through the drawers and cupboards in the kitchen. I put all the food in one of the bags. Thankfully someone had cleaned out the fridge. The dishes and utensils could stay where they were for now. I went upstairs and went through the bedrooms in the same fashion, taking things downstairs to the appropriate pile. I left the bedding where it was and piled any extra bedding on the beds.

I did all of this in about an hour. I closed most of the windows, but left the doors open for a while, and decided to look around to see if I missed anything.

I went into what looked like Simpson's bedroom. There was wall-to-wall carpet in the bedroom and a loose rug covering the floor in the spacious closet. I didn't see anything in the bedroom, so I went in the closet that I had previously quickly emptied. As I stepped on the rug, I heard a squeak from the flooring that I had been too busy to notice before. My mind went to work before I could bend down and move the rug, wondering if there might be something hidden under the flooring.

I lifted the rug and set it out of the way in the bedroom and looked at the flooring. There were no obvious loose boards. I stepped on them until I found the one that had squeaked. I stepped on it a few times to see if it would move. It did. I looked more closely and could see small scratches at one end. Using my fingernails, I got a hold of that end, and lifted it up. As I did, I noticed several other boards move. When I took all the loose boards out, I found stacks of cash, a few shiny, small bars of gold, and banking information, including usernames and passwords for on-line access.

There were twenty stacks of hundreds and a few stacks of fiftys and twentys. All were wrapped in bank wrappers. I made a quick count of the cash and it came to two-hundred fifty thousand five hundred dollars. I had no way to estimate the value of the gold or to verify the bank account at this point.

What the hell? How had this sad, angry old man come up with all this money? Where did it come from? Was it connected to something illegal? I wouldn't get any answers sitting on the floor of the bedroom, and all of the money had to be cleared out before anyone else came in.

I packed all the cash in one of the black plastic bags. I put the bank information into an empty envelope I found and tossed it into the bag with the money. I carried the bag out to my SUV, and then came back for the gold. I looked under the floor more carefully and found two more bars for a total of five. I put them in the back of the SUV and covered them up. I closed the rest of the house windows, locked the doors, and sat on the front step to catch my breath. Then I called Frank Wilkins.

"Frank, we need to talk with Rachael."

4.

I was still sitting on the front step when Frank called me back with a time for meeting with Rachael. It would be in an hour in Frank's office in Tipton. When I arrived I asked him if I could arrange what I had found on a table in the meeting room. His next client appointment was in the afternoon, so he helped me.

We stacked the cash on the end of the table. When Frank got over the shock of seeing so much cash, he said that the gold bars were smaller than the standard ingot, and then weighed each on his office scale. We had to convert the answer to Troy ounces and arrived at three Troy ounces per bar. At the current price of gold the value of each bar was worth close to five thousand dollars. I didn't want to risk connecting to the bank online to get a current balance until I could do it safely. The latest bank statement put the balance at five hundred thousand and change.

"What do we have here, Frank?" I asked when we sat down and looked at the treasure I had uncovered. Frank was older than when he helped me all those years before, but still only about sixty. He was five nine and weighed around one seventy. It looked like he had kept fit over the years. What was left of his black hair was mostly gray now. He was still professional in his manner and had a welcoming smile.

"I don't know anything about any of this," he said. "I doubt anyone in town ever thought there could be this much money in Simpson's run-down shack."

"Easy there," I smiled. "I own that shack now, but I know what you mean."

Frank picked up a stack of twentys and looked at the words on the wrappers that were on all of the stacks.

"I don't recognize the bank named on this wrapper. Hang on a minute."

He went to his workstation and took a few minutes looking up the name of the bank that was on the wrappers. When he found it, he searched for additional information about it.

"Delta National Bank was a one-town bank in a small town in Mississippi."

"Was?" I queried.

"Yes, it went out of business thirty years ago."

"Did they merge with a larger bank?"

"No. It seems they just went out of business. It had been owned and run by a family there, and they just closed the bank. There was some controversy, but nothing about the depositors losing money. I imagine that the mortgages and other loans were transferred to other institutions."

"So the stacks of cash in front of us may have come through there at some time, but there is no indication that it was obtained illegally?"

"None that I can see," Frank confirmed.

"We won't have to tell Rachael that her father robbed the bank," I said, "but we don't have the answers we need. Maybe she has some information that would shed some light on all of this."

"Could be. We'll know in a minute or two," Frank said. He was looking out the window. "She's coming to the door now."

Frank went out to greet Rachael. When he brought her in, she said, "Nice to see you again, Tom." She didn't react to the money but sat as far away from it as she could.

Rachael had been in my class in high school. She was a good student, but always seemed sad and kept to herself. She smiled more now, but the sadness of those earlier years was still in her eyes.

"What do we have here?" Rachael asked.

On the phone, Frank had told her that I had found some money in the house but not the amount. Her eyes became larger in stages as she took in all that was in front of her. I let Frank do the talking.

"There is nearly three hundred thousand in cash and gold on the table. There's a bank statement which indicates that there may be another five hundred thousand in the account, but we haven't confirmed that."

"It's not mine," Rachael said, turning to me. "You bought the house, Tom. It's yours."

"I don't see it that way, Rachael," I said, in the gentlest voice I could manage. I could see that this was bringing up unpleasant memories.

"It's true, I did buy the place, but this money wasn't part of the deal," I said. "It belongs to you."

"I don't want it!" Rachael blurted out.

We let things settle down before going further. We didn't want to push. It was easy to see that this was hard for her. Frank picked up the conversation again after a bit.

"We understand, Rachael," he said. "If we could set aside who owns it for a minute, Tom and I were wondering if you had any clue that might help us determine where all of this came from."

"Before we go into that," she said more composed, "first let me apologize for my outburst. I don't know anything about the money and I truly do not want it. Tom, you gave me a very fair price for the place, more than I expected. I have enough money for my needs. I have no need for anything on this table or in that bank.

"Besides not needing it," she continued, "I don't want the attention that it will draw. I can imagine that the money wasn't gained legally. Those connected to it might come looking for it. In addition, there's the government. They'll want to know where it came from. I don't know the answer, and I don't want to know."

I admired Rachael for her reasoned response to what was a very emotional situation. We asked a few more questions, and then Frank said, "I understand you don't want this money, Rachael. I doubt you will change your mind, but we won't be doing anything with it for a while in case you do."

"Thanks, Frank," she said. She got up from the table. She stood up to her full height, squared her shoulders, and with a proud and determined look on her face said, "I appreciate the way you and Tom have handled this, but I will *never* touch any of that money!" She turned and left the office without another word.

5.

Frank and I watched Rachael leave, and then turned to each other.

"That woman has been through a lot in her life," Frank said. "All her troubles haven't defeated her. I'm glad to see it."

"I always felt sorry for her when we were in school together. It's good to see that she has made a life for herself. It's clear that she doesn't want any of this." I said waving my arm taking in all that was on the table. "Where does that leave us?"

"Us?" Frank asked smiling. "My only connection to all of this is that *your* money is on *my* table. I'd appreciate it if you'd clear it all out before someone sees it."

"Right."

Frank laughed and said, "You know I'll try to help you where I can, Tom. Rachael was right when she said this treasure trove will draw attention of one kind or another. Even if Simpson's hypothetical partners in crime don't show up, the government will when you deposit this much cash in a bank. Any cash deposit of ten thousand or more must be reported to the Feds and this much will definitely get their attention. When the Feds learn of the bank account you found they'll be even more interested, and they will have questions. I think it's likely that you will be constrained as to what you can do with the money until they've investigated where it came from. That might take them a long time. They'll be suspicious of you, and you will be under scrutiny the entire time."

"I won't be the only one investigated," I said. "If we trigger the attention of the government, they'll probably also ask Rachael questions. Still, it might be better to contact the appropriate government office and tell them what I have found. We'll still get the questions but calling them ahead of time might reduce the suspicion."

"That might be best," Frank said. "If we decide to do that, we should warn Rachael. Maybe you can be with Rachel if the government wants to ask her questions. Let's think about it for a while."

"What do we do with this stash in the meantime?"

"I have a large safe in the back. Let's put it there until we decide."

I helped Frank move the cash and gold to his safe. I kept the information for that strange bank account. I wanted to know more about it before we took the next step.

I thanked Frank and left. A few doors down Main Street from Frank's office there was a second-hand store called Manny's. I went in and asked the owner if he would like the furniture, dishes and things from the house. He asked what I wanted for it. I told him nothing. He liked the price. He said he could be out there shortly after lunch.

I visited a thrift shop a couple of blocks away. They were interested in the clothes but didn't have a way to pick them up. I said I would be glad to deliver them.

I went to the local hardware store and bought some packing supplies. I didn't want the dishes to be left behind because Manny didn't have anything to put them in. Then I drove out to the house and started packing the clothes into the SUV. Manny and his help arrived just as I finished removing the last of the clothes.

Manny's eyes lit up when he saw what I had to give him. He had his men start taking the furniture out. His wife had come along and started using the materials I had brought to pack everything. I asked them to take the bedding along with the beds and said that I would pick it up later. Manny didn't mind. In fact he hardly thought about it at all. Manny was focused on the junk that I had piled in the corner. He ended up taking most of it with him.

In a few hours, the house was nearly empty. Manny and his crew were gone. I put the remaining items, bags of food and trash, into my SUV. I walked through the house and closed all of the windows. As I was going out the front door, I turned, took a deep breath, and opened my senses. I sensed nothing of old man Simpson. He was gone!

I drove back to town and dropped off the clothing at the thrift shop. When I stopped by Manny's to pick up the bedding, I asked if I could throw the trash in his dumpster out back. He nodded that I could, as he was trying to figure out where to put the treasures he had picked up at my place. Then I drove to a nearby homeless shelter and gave them the bedding and food.

I went out to my SUV and looked inside. It was as empty as the house. Not bad for one day's work.

It was getting dark when I arrived at the Boarding House. There wasn't a separate parking place attached to the house, but there was plenty of room on the street.

I had always thought the Boarding House was nice when I was a kid. The front yard was filled with a planting area that had blooms of all kinds in the Spring and Summer. Everything was in great shape. The outside was painted cream white with forest green trim. It had a large wrap-around porch with chairs for sitting outside in warmer weather. It looked welcoming as I came up to the front steps.

The inside had been upgraded over the years, but the better pieces of furniture from the past had been kept, providing a comfortable place for the boarders to relax downstairs. The rooms upstairs were well furnished, but small as one would expect given the overall size and age of the building. Each had its own bathroom, which was good, especially for a longer-term stay.

Eleanor was in the hall when I came in.

"Hi, Tom. You left early this morning. Missed breakfast."

"I went to Mel's this morning. I'll be at your table tomorrow morning."

"What did you do all day?"

"I exorcised a ghost."

Eleanor gave me a you-need-to-explain-that-one look.

"I cleaned everything out of the house, ridding the place of any presence of the previous owner."

"That was fast."

"It needed to be done right away."

"I understand, Tom."

Eleanor had some linens in her arms, and was on her way to somewhere in the house when I came in. I didn't want to keep her.

"I'm sorry about missing dinner last night. I'll be there tonight."

She smiled and said, "I'm glad to hear that. You are the only boarder right now, so that will give us a chance to catch up."

Her smile still had that effect on me. I felt all warm inside.

"See you then," I said.

She smiled again and went on her way. I went upstairs to my room, sat down, and calmed myself. It wasn't like me to be so affected by talking to a woman, but for me there was always a magic surrounding Eleanor. I'm glad I felt it, but it was disquieting all the same.

6.

I felt relaxed after taking a shower and putting on a dark-green cotton turtleneck with clean jeans. There was about an hour before dinner. I thought I'd use the time to investigate the bank account that I'd found with the money.

I didn't want to try to log onto the bank directly until I knew more about it. I looked at the bank statement more closely. The name at the top of the statement was Perrin International Banking, but no address, phone number or other information was provided. That was mysterious, maybe even dodgy.

Using my laptop, I routed my search through several proxy servers I had used in the past, hoping that would be safe enough. After a substantial amount of digging, I found one obscure reference to Perrin International Banking. I got the impression that it didn't have an address—that it existed only in cyber space.

I didn't need to know anything more. I covered my tracks and shut down my laptop. I may have triggered something by looking up the name, but I couldn't do anything about it. I put the bank information back in the envelope and set it aside. The bank account had been idle for years. As far as I was concerned it would remain that way.

I went downstairs, drawn by the smell of Eleanor's cooking. I passed by the kitchen on my way toward the dining room.

"There's some red wine open on the bureau," Eleanor said. "Why don't you have a glass while I finish up here."

"I'll do that. What are we having?"

"Something that goes well with red wine," she said, sounding rushed and impatient. "Now go on."

I looked forward to whatever smelled so good. I poured the red wine in the crystal goblet provided and took a sip. I'm not a wine expert. For me if a wine tastes good, it's a good wine. This red blend tasted good.

With my wine in hand I looked around the room. In the center was a large, rectangular, wood dining table with eight chairs around it. Tonight, there were just two place settings, across from each other near one end of the table. There were two extra chairs in separate corners. The only other furniture in the room was the old and ornately crafted bureau that the wine was on. It was stained dark brown and looked to be of fine workmanship. I couldn't see much of the dining table under the tablecloth. What I could see looked like it was made at the same time as the bureau and with the same care.

On the walls were pictures that covered a period before the house had become Mrs. Jorgensen's Boarding House. One of the older pictures showed the place with a sign out front that simply said, "Rooms for Rent." It looked like it might have started out as a boarding house rather than a single-family home. There were other pictures of what were probably noteworthy guests, but I didn't recognize any of them.

More recent pictures were of Eleanor's family. Eleanor and her brother Billy were in most of them. There was a man with Eleanor's mother in some of the pictures that was likely Eleanor's father. I knew of him but had never met him. He died in an accident at the Mill when I was young.

Eleanor came in with a basket of bread and a steaming bowl of pasta with vegetables in a red sauce. She set the basket on the table and the bowl on a ceramic trivet she had put on the table before.

"Dinner is served," she said.

She motioned for me to sit at one of the places previously set and sat across from me. She looked flustered from all the last-minute preparations. She took a deep breath, immediately calming herself. She smiled and said, "I hope you like the sauce on the pasta."

I leaned forward and inhaled the aroma of the pasta dish.

"It smells wonderful! Thank you."

Eleanor watched Tom eating and wondered why she found herself smiling every time she looked at him since he had arrived unexpectedly two nights ago. She smiled occasionally during the day normally. It was her nature. The feeling she had when she smiled at Tom was coming from something deep inside her.

It was nice to see Tom again, but there was more here than seeing an old school friend. She had thought about him occasionally after he left, but those thoughts had passed quickly. When he came through the door and asked for a room, it was like a missing piece of a puzzle fell into place. When she saw his reaction to her, the way he seemed to catch his breath, she smiled even more.

"Apparently the food is okay," she said.

I had just taken another bite of pasta so all I could manage in response was nodding my head up and down vigorously and making an appreciative noise with my mouth closed. Having taken the edge off my hunger I slowed down.

"It's great, Eleanor. If you do the cooking for your boarders, I'll bet you get a lot of repeat business."

“I do some of the cooking, but Betty Saunders does some as well.”

“Mrs. Saunders, as in Jimmy’s mom?”

“Yes, she’s been helping me for a few years now.”

When I looked like I could use an explanation, Eleanor continued.

“Business at the Mill was slowing down, and it eventually got so slow that the Mill closed completely. Mr. Saunders became despondent and died from an overdose a few years later. Betty had some money, but she needed to supplement what she had, and needed something to do.

“She’s been great. She normally eats dinner here, but tonight she chose to eat at her place. I didn’t say anything, but when I was talking about eating with you tonight, I think she got the impression we wanted to catch up. Also having to explain why she was working here would have been awkward for her. She probably guessed that I’d tell you, and then the topic wouldn’t have to come up.”

It was nice to be with Eleanor. Her smiling at me while I was sitting down was easier to handle. Since I was sitting down, I didn’t have to worry about my knees failing me. So I could carry on a conversation more easily.

“It must have been tough for Mrs. Saunders the way Jimmy went and then her husband. How’s she doing?”

“I think she’s doing better as a person than all of the time she was married. Mr. Saunders ran his household like he ran the Mill, barking out orders. So, yes, I think Betty is doing well, making a life for herself.”

I didn’t know where to go next so I thought talking about the weather might be good. Apparently Eleanor was having the same problem because she brought up the weather. Since I couldn’t use the weather, I started “catching up.”

"How have you been, Eleanor? You look great. Running this place must agree with you."

"This is the life I've always known, and it suits me. I like meeting people who stay here. Fewer people are coming here since the Mill closed, but business is still doing okay. It was hard for me when I lost Mom, but I worked my way through that. I'm fine now. How about you? What do you have to say for yourself, 'Mr. gone for fifteen years'?"

I wanted Eleanor to know more about what I'd done, so I gave her more details.

"So you're a man of means."

"Yes, but I don't want to make a big deal out of it. I think knowing that I have money would cause people to treat me differently. That would get in the way. So if you could keep it to yourself, I'd appreciate it."

"So are you planning to stay here, now that you have bought the land out on Tyler road?"

"I think I'd like to, but I'll have to see how it goes. I'll need somewhere to stay until I get a place of my own set up. I'd like to keep a room here during that time."

She laughed and waved her hand around at the empty dining room and in the gesture included the whole building. "As you can see, I think we can accommodate you."

"Well, I'm glad you can work me in."

We had some more wine and talked about various things including times at school. After a couple of hours I stood and said, "Let me help you clear the table."

We talked some more as we brought things into the kitchen. Eventually it was time to call it a night.

I said good night to Eleanor, and I went up to my room. It had been a full day and a pleasant evening with Eleanor. I was ready for a good night's sleep. It wasn't to be.

About midnight I was awakened by a determined and incessant knocking. It wasn't at the door as I would have expected. Someone was knocking on the window, and it sounded odd.

I got up and slipped on my jeans and a shirt. I went over to the window. My room was on the second floor and faced the back of the Boarding House. It would have been too dark to see much out of the window but there was a streetlight, which shined in my direction.

I couldn't make sense out of what I was seeing. There was a shiny metal arm about an inch thick with a joint in the middle and a knob on the end. The arm was knocking the knob against the window. The oddest thing was that the arm wasn't connected to anything. It appeared to be floating by itself in midair!

7.

Shortly after I arrived at the window, the knocking stopped. The arm began moving in a different way. It would point at me and then point down. It pointed at me three times, and then pointed down. I got the point. The arm wanted me to go downstairs and into the backyard.

I surmised that the arm wasn't acting on its own. Instead it seemed my new friend, the vehicle that I found in the forest, came back in its invisible form, and was asking me to meet it in the backyard. It had seemed harmless enough in our first encounter when it wanted out of my barn. Besides I was curious. I put the rest of my clothes on with boots and a jacket and went to visit with the unknown.

I went down the stairs and to the front door as quietly as I could. I had a key to the front door so I could lock it as I went out. Not so with the back door. I didn't want to leave any door unlocked even for a few minutes. This might take time to sort out especially if we were going to depend on sign language using a mechanical arm.

The backyard was fenced, but the gate wasn't locked. Several sitting areas had been arranged for use by the guests. There was an open area on the grass, where I thought the invisible vehicle might be. I thought it might take some time to find it. I was wrong.

As I stepped closer, what I guessed was the front door of the vehicle opened. There was a dim light coming from inside. The intent was clear. It wanted me to get inside.

I paused. In the short time since I discovered the vehicle, I had learned nothing about it. It didn't appear to be aggressive, but that didn't mean it was harmless. The interior light blinked insistently when I didn't go right in. I thought I'd better get this over with before we drew unwanted attention from neighbors.

I entered and sat down. The door closed and the seat adjusted itself to fit my torso. There was no noise, but I felt the vehicle rise. I didn't know how fast or how far because there were no windows to see outside. Then I figured it out. It wouldn't be invisible if the interior lights could be seen. Still it was disorienting to be moving and not being able to see outside.

A screen came on in front of me. Words began to stream across the screen. They were in English, which given the setting was a bit of a surprise.

On the screen the machine said, "Sorry for the clandestine approach to this meeting, but I thought it was important to not be detected. So I came at night and chose to be invisible."

"Can you understand me if I speak out loud?" I asked.

"Yes," came on the screen.

"Why did you want to meet with me?"

"I needed to communicate with you, and there was no other way. I had to get you inside so you could see the screen."

"Okay, I'm here. Wait. Where are we?"

"Ten thousand feet above where I picked you up."

I had barely felt the lift. Interesting, but a topic for another time.

"What did you want to say?"

There was a long pause, and I just waited. Maybe it had a reason to be hesitant.

"I need to accept your offer of residing in your barn. It might be for an indefinite period."

There was something it wasn't telling me. I didn't want to push too much, but if it was going to be my guest for a while, we were going to have to get to know each other.

"My offer still stands. Can you tell me why you think it will be for a longer time?"

"I was damaged when I crashed in your forest. My interstellar flight capability is not functioning. I do not know if I can repair it. I need a safe place to stay until I can determine what to do. Besides a place, I need…a friend."

That got to me. I wasn't communicating with a computer. Inside this machine was a sophisticated, self-aware intelligence, and it wanted me to be its friend.

"Thank you for seeking me out to be your friend, but why me? There are over eight billion humans on this planet."

"True. If I had met someone else, they might have been as understanding as you, but I liked the way you did not ask questions. Encountering me was a very unusual experience for you. You could have tried to keep me in your barn. Instead, even without being able to communicate with me, you treated me as an individual with the right of self-determination. I liked that very much.

When I learned that I was going to be here for some time, I hoped I could continue to depend upon your good nature. I need someone to communicate with, maybe work with while I am here. Perhaps I could help you in some way. I might ask you for help. Right now, I am asking you for your friendship."

"I may have merely been trying to let a wild machine out to keep it from damaging my barn."

"You tried to warn me of the dangers," it said. "I did not understand the words, but I could determine your intent. I tried to ease your concern by showing you I could become invisible. I recorded the words and when I became proficient in English, I translated them and learned the specific dangers you were alerting me to.

"Once I understood I was going to be here for a while, I connected to your world network. I learned as much as I could about this world. I have learned languages. I have researched you, your past activities, and your current interactions on the network. I found you to be a good representative of your race."

What could I say to all of that? An intelligent visitor from an advanced civilization surveyed my world. When it was done it asked *me* to be its friend. It felt odd to have been investigated like that, but it didn't matter.

"Thank you. I am honored and will be glad to be your friend. What can I do for you?"

A tray slid out of the panel in front of me. There was a small patch of something resting on it.

"What's that?"

"That is the way we can communicate so I won't have to knock on your window in the middle of the night. A communication device is on the back of the patch. You apply the patch to your skin behind and below your ear. Tiny machines you would call nanites will implant the device and attach it to your nervous system. Then you can communicate with me. You can talk to me or you can simply think what you want to communicate, and I will receive it just the same. It will also convey visual images you want me to see."

That was a lot to take in. I had questions.

"I'm concerned about several things," I said. "Will it damage my nervous system? After all, you are not familiar with my physiology. Will you be listening to me when I'm not communicating with you? Is this something you can use to control me in some way?"

"I understand," it said. "The answer to all three of the concerns you listed is, 'no.' In addition once it is installed you can eliminate it just by thinking that you don't want it anymore. The device and all connections to your system will dissolve and be washed out of your body."

I said I'd be his friend. If he wanted to do me harm, there were much easier ways of doing that. I picked up the patch and placed it where he said. I felt a small tingle where I had placed it and then nothing. I gave it a few minutes to settle in, and then tried it out. It could already hear me in the cabin without the device, so I thought something at it.

"Is this working?" I asked.

"Yes," it answered. Only I didn't hear the answer with my ears. I received the answer in the same way I had transmitted. I received its thought. Hmmm.

"This is like telepathy," I said.

"Yes, but more discrete and more dependable. I can only hear the thoughts you transmit, and they come through clearly every time. Also, it has a visual component."

A moment later, it showed me a visual of myself. I "saw" my face as clearly as if I were looking in a mirror.

"This will take getting used to," I said out loud, mostly to myself.

"It will seem natural very soon. The challenge might be when communicating with others to remember that they do not have one of these."

"What's next…? Wait. I don't know what to call you. Do you have a name?"

"Not a name exactly. I have a role and a unit number. In your number system, I am number twenty-seven."

"I don't want to call you 'Twenty-Seven.' Maybe there is something in what you do that we can use. What is your job?"

“Roughly translated into English I am Galactic Exploration and Research Intelligence number twenty-seven.”

“The first letter of those words comes out G.E.R.I., so I’ll call you GERI if that’s okay.

“That is acceptable.”

“Okay, what’s next GERI?”

“There is one more thing before we’re done for tonight.”

“What’s that?”

“Your inquiry into Perrin International Banking tripped an alert.”

8.

Eleanor looked at Tom as he came into the kitchen for breakfast. He was wearing the same green turtleneck and jeans as last night. He looked bigger and stronger than he did in high school. This morning his dark brown hair had defied his attempt to get it under control. His tanned face contained eyes that looked like they didn't get enough sleep. He might have had a rough night, but he had some explaining to do.

"Who's your friend?" she asked, with a mischievous smile.

I looked around to see who Eleanor was referring to. Then it hit me. She was talking about last night.

I couldn't get to sleep for hours thinking about GERI and what being his "friend" would mean. GERI had said that the alert my search had triggered hadn't been acted upon, and that he would notify me if something else happened. Still it was unsettling and would need to be addressed. Things had become complicated. Eleanor's question upped the level of complexity.

"Ummm," I said.

"I have lived in this house my whole life, Tom. I know all its noises and when some noise is unusual like last night. I heard rapping on a window. Then I heard my only boarder leave by the front door and go into the backyard. When I looked out my window, I saw what looked like a small car door open in midair and you step in. Then you, the door and everything disappeared. 'Ummm' doesn't quite explain all of that, Tom Williams."

We both laughed. I liked Eleanor. She deserved an explanation, but would knowing everything put her in danger? Of course my being here may have already put her in danger. She would be better off if she knew.

"Why don't we talk things over while we eat?"

She had made some pancakes and put them in the middle of the table. I sat down put a couple on my plate. She did the same. I applied butter and syrup, took a bite, and started talking.

"Eleanor, I bought the Simpson place because I've always wanted the forest on that land. I got more than I bargained for. Tuesday, I went out there to take a walk in the forest and I found something. That something has become as you say my 'friend.'"

I told her about finding and releasing GERI, what the name GERI meant, and his return which she had witnessed last night. I told her everything, including my new implanted, hi-tech communication device.

"Amazing, Tom. If I hadn't seen what I saw last night I wouldn't be able to believe any of it. Now that I know about it, I don't know what to do."

"You're the only one who knows, Eleanor. I need to keep it that way. Can you live with keeping GERI a secret?"

"Of course, Tom, but still…"

"I understand. I need to sort it out. I'll keep you posted. There's more."

"What? Are there two of them?" she asked. "Are we being invaded?"

I laughed, but it was an understandable question given what she had just learned.

"No, there is only one GERI. It's something else. On Wednesday, when I let GERI out of the barn, I started the process of cleaning out the house. I found a ton of money under the floor in old Simpson's closet."

"It sounds like you think that is a bad thing."

"There were stacks of hundred's, fifty's and twenty's in bank wrappers. Also, there were several small gold bars and a bank statement. The cash and bars come to nearly three-hundred thousand dollars. The bank account appears to have another five-hundred thousand."

"That's a lot of money, Tom."

"It is. I didn't think it was right that I should keep it. I asked Frank Wilkins to set up a meeting with Rachael so I could give it to her."

"What did she say?"

"She was very clear that she wanted nothing to do with the money."

"I can understand her reaction," Eleanor said. "She didn't talk much in school, but one time she broke down and cried. I asked her what was wrong, and she told me about her father's abuse and mistreatment of her and her mother. Having that money would be a reminder of her terrible ordeal."

"There was that," I said, "but she also pointed out that it might have been obtained illegally and someone might come looking for it. Whether or not it's illegal, the government will want to know where it came from. She didn't want to face all of their questions."

"So what did you do?"

"Frank and I put the cash and gold in his safe. I took the bank information to see what I could find out. Last night before our dinner together, I looked up the name of the bank. The whole thing looked dodgy. There was no reason to take a risk looking into it, so I decided to stop looking. Apparently it won't end that easily."

"What do you mean?"

"My computer search of the bank name triggered something. Some government agency set a watch on anything connected with that bank's name."

"How do you know that? Did they contact you?"

"No. GERI told me."

Eleanor sat back with wide eyes. I told her what I knew of GERI's connecting to the web, learning about our world, and investigating me. I worried that this was getting to be too much for her. I needn't have.

"That can be useful, Tom, if GERI is really your friend," she said.

"Yes."

"Is there more to your story?" Eleanor asked.

"No. That's it so far."

I thought for a moment before I launched into what was on my mind. Apparently she guessed I had something else to say.

"What is it, Tom?"

"I'm concerned about what all this means for you. I'm staying in your house. I don't want to bring trouble to your doorstep."

"What kind of trouble?"

"The money for starters. There may be some criminals in the mix, but at the very least, the government will be looking into this."

"I can handle that."

"I am sure you can Eleanor, but what about your other boarders?"

"I'm lucky to get three in a month from October through March."

"Do you have any bookings?"

"No, but some might come up around Thanksgiving or as we get closer to Christmas."

"I would really like to stay here, but I don't want it to be a problem for you financially or otherwise. Please don't be offended, but how about if I rent your place until Thanksgiving."

"What, the entire place?"

"Yes."

"Besides being expensive, I wouldn't normally have that many boarders."

"Okay, let me pay the equivalent of three boarders from now until Thanksgiving, and don't take any other bookings for that period."

"That's a lot of money, Tom. You don't need to do that."

I could see her thinking about what it would be like if she didn't take my offer and didn't take on any other boarders until Thanksgiving. It wouldn't work.

"If I didn't have any boarders but you, my expenses would be lower. It would work if you paid for your room plus one other room during that time."

"Works for me. Just charge the card I gave you when I checked in, for the entire period up front. Wait, what about Mrs. Saunders and others you would normally have help you?"

"I'll call Betty. I'll ask her to let me pay her for the period I won't be open. I hope she will accept it. She's the only one I have helping me this time of the year."

"Won't she be curious, and talk with others about it?"

"She'll be curious, but she'll be thinking that I've decided that I need more time "catching up" with you. She will be discrete about it."

I saw Eleanor blush when she considered what she had just said. I think I did too. We both went back to our pancakes. They had gone cold during our talk, but that wasn't a problem. We needed a moment. I tried to ease past the awkwardness.

"It will be nice to have more time to talk," I said. "I'll try to keep my recent discoveries from being a problem for you."

"Thanks, but I think we can handle what comes up. What will you do next?"

"I think the best thing is to contact the FBI to let them know what I have found. They may not be the agency that is watching the bank, but I will be on the record as bringing the situation to the government instead of them having to come to me."

"Good idea."

We talked some more about the money and GERI. After breakfast, I offered to help clean up.

"You are a boarder, Tom," she said, smiling. "You go do your things. I'll do mine. Usually I change the bedding every other day. Will that suit you?"

I smiled back. "Yes. I'll try to keep my room orderly."

"I expect nothing less."

Our eyes met. We laughed at our formality, but we knew it would be a good idea to continue with the usual boarder routine. Because…well, we just knew it would be better.

I first called Rachel to tell her I was going to the FBI with the money. She wasn't happy, but she also thought it was best. I offered to be with her if they needed to ask her questions. She thanked me for that.

Then I contacted the FBI. They had an office in Seattle which was about a ninety-minute drive to the south. I was connected to Agent Riley Thomas. She seemed bored when I said I had found some money. She became more interested when I described the wrapped bundles of bills and gold. She really perked up when I told her about the odd bank account.

"Can you bring all of that into our office?" she asked. "I'd be fine coming to you, but I think we will want to use our systems right away to examine the wrapped bills."

"I can be there today," I said. "What time?"

We set the time for 10:30 that morning.

"How will this work?" I asked.

"What do you mean?"

"I'll be bringing a large, black plastic bag with a bunch of money in it to your front door. That might be a bit awkward."

Agent Thomas laughed at the image. "Call when you arrive. I'll come down."

9.

I asked Frank to meet me at his office. It was early for him, but he didn't complain. He seemed happy to have the money removed from his safe. Then I made the drive to Seattle in my SUV. On the way, GERI told me through my implant that the FBI acted on the alert my search triggered and traced the inquiry to me. I thought it would be a good idea to act surprised when it came up.

It was a cloudy, cold wet October day so the Emerald City wasn't shining. The FBI was in a tall building between Seneca and Spring on Third Street. I parked in the underground parking and took the elevator to the ground floor. As I expected Security was uncomfortable with my black plastic bag.

They called Agent Thomas, and she arrived in a few minutes. She was wearing a brown jacket and matching pants. She was about five-foot ten and had a slender build. The dark green blouse she wore highlighted her light complexion, and her gray-green eyes. Her dark brown hair was cut short. She was all business when she talked with Security. They weren't feeling much better, but they did let me and my bag into the building.

We rode the elevator up to the floor where her office was and went into a separate meeting room. The open area and offices looked functional, but uninteresting. The meeting room was about the same. I took the bag to the table, and carefully let the money and the gold slide out onto the table. I stacked the money and put the gold bars next to the stacks. I had kept out the Perrin bank account number, the username and password and had left that information in my room. I was pretty sure I would never need it, but I've been wrong about that kind of thing before.

Agent Thomas wasn't one for small talk. Neither was I.

"You are right about the bank name on the wrappers," she said. "Delta National went out of business thirty years ago. There is no record of it being robbed. When I read about the closure it seemed odd, but I couldn't identify anything concrete."

"What about Perrin International Banking?" I asked.

"There is an old file with that name on it which was nearly empty. The agent who initiated the inquiry worked in our Memphis office. All he put in the file was that he was to be notified if anything came up with that name on it. He retired thirteen years ago, but the Bureau never forgets. It never drops a case until it's done one way or the other. We've been watching that bank's name for thirty years. Yesterday, it came up on the grid."

"That was probably me," I said. "I didn't do much. I just looked up the name. When I found it, I got right back out."

"I saw yours," she said.

"What do you mean?"

"Just what I said. Your search was noted."

"You could tell it was me? I thought I hid my tracks."

"You did a fairly good job of it, but our system is able to trace through to the originator in many situations. We saw that yours was simply a name look up. We would have contacted you to ask you why you were interested. It was better that you came in.

"We were not able to trace the other ping that came up on the bank name. It also happened yesterday."

"What was the other ping?"

"It looked like an echo."

"An echo?"

"A reflexive response to your inquiry. Your inquiry caused a message to be sent noting that someone was interested in Perrin. We couldn't find what created the echo, or where the message was sent. I would guess something that sophisticated could also have identified the person who made the inquiry and that person's location. You might be contacted by someone. We need you to let us know if that happens."

What had I stumbled into? This did not sound good. I'd better prepare, and let Eleanor know. Maybe GERI could help. I had asked him to listen in and record everything that occurred at the FBI this morning.

"GERI did you get all that?" I thought at him through my implant while Agent Thomas was counting the money.

"Yes, I did, Tom. I'll see what I can find out."

"Thanks."

"Mr. Williams?"

"Huh? Oh, sorry. I missed your question."

"I didn't ask a question. I said that I was leaving the room to have an official receipt made up for what you have brought to the office."

"You're keeping it?"

"Yes. Until we can determine if the money is connected to anything the Bureau should be interested in. Is that a problem?"

"No. Actually I'm glad to put it in your hands. At least until this is all cleared up."

She nodded and said, "I'll be right back."

I was happy to be rid of the money. I had hoped that would be the end of it. I would leave the money with them and walk away. It probably would take the FBI forever to investigate it before they gave me a call. They might say something was wrong, and they needed to keep it until their investigation was complete. If they said I could have it back, at least having had the FBI investigate it, might reduce the questions from the Feds when I deposited it in my bank account. With the other alert my inquiry had set off, it might not end so simply.

Agent Thomas came back in and handed me the receipt. It looked correct. I asked that she also send me an email with the receipt attached. I might lose the paper and wouldn't be able to prove I'd given her the money. I thought an email would help. Of course, I also had GERI's recording as back up.

"Now tell me more about how you found the money," she said.

I told her the whole story. It didn't take long.

"The daughter says she knows nothing about the money?" Agent Thomas asked.

"That's right and she doesn't want it."

When the agent was surprised, I told her the little I knew about the family situation.

"I understand," Thomas said.

It looked like she really did understand. Maybe she'd seen similar situations or maybe it was more personal.

"If you want to ask Rachael Simpson questions, I would like to be there for support. She really doesn't want anything to do with this."

"I'll keep that in mind if we go in that direction. I have no other questions at this time. Do you?"

"Nope."

I got up to leave.

"We'll let you know if we find something, or if we need to talk with you again."

I left and headed home.

By the time I was leaving the northern edge of Seattle on I-5, GERI contacted me.

"Blackwell Textiles, in Darlynn, South Carolina," he said. "That's the name of the company that received the message about your inquiry."

"Has anyone picked up on it?" I asked.

"No. They may not do anything."

"Why not?"

"Blackwell Textiles was established before your Civil War. They stopped operating thirty years ago. The building is still there, but the textile mill is idle."

Thirty years ago. Could it just be a coincidence that Delta National also closed thirty years ago. I didn't think so.

"They may no longer be making fabric," I said, "but if what Agent Thomas said is accurate, there is modern and sophisticated information technology operating there. Doesn't that strike you as odd?"

"I'm not familiar enough with things on your world to determine if it is 'odd,'" GERI answered. "However, I do not understand why such equipment would be in a building that is otherwise not being used."

"On this world most people would call that 'odd.'"

"Thank you," GERI said.

"It is also mysterious since that someone there is still interested in anything to do with this unusual bank."

"I'll monitor the situation and let you know if anything else occurs."

"Thanks."

I called Rachel. I told her what had happened with the FBI. I said that Agent Thomas did not need to talk with her at this time. She was relieved.

When I drove up in front of the Boarding House, there was a man talking with Eleanor at the front door. It didn't look like a friendly discussion. I quickly parked and went to see what was going on.

"I am not renting any rooms at this time, period, Mr. Trotter," Eleanor said, as I came up by the door.

The man looked at me. I sent a visual image to GERI and asked him to investigate this man who apparently was giving Eleanor a bad time. He looked to be about fifty years old. He was five-foot seven at the most. He weighed more than he should and more than he did when he bought the odd colored brown suit he was wearing. His face was pudgy. He was being rude and aggressive.

"Hi, Eleanor," I said. "What's going on?"

"Mr. Trotter is asking to rent a room. He won't take 'no' for an answer."

I turned to the man and said, "That's the end of the conversation, Mr. Trotter. You'll have to find a room somewhere else. There's a Day's Inn about three miles west of town. That's the closest place."

"I wasn't talking to you, friend," Trotter said, and turned to have another go at Eleanor.

I stepped between him and Eleanor.

"True, but I was talking to you. I'm not your friend, but I was trying to be friendly. You should move on now."

He tried to push me out of the way. That was a mistake. When I was in the Air Force, they thought that the top-secret subjects I was working on could put me in dangerous situations, so they put me through extensive self-defense and hand-to-hand combat training. I got the feeling that the Air Force wasn't concerned about me. They just were trying to keep me from being captured by someone who wanted our "secrets."

Whatever their reason, I was glad to have the training. It helped in situations like this one.

I grabbed Trotter's left hand which he was using in his attempt to move me out of the way. I twisted it in a way that was painful for him, and quickly drew it and his left arm behind his back. When I added a little pressure he complained.

"Ow! What the hell do you think you are doing?" he asked, through gritted teeth.

"Defending myself and attempting to persuade you to leave. Let's go find your car, shall we?"

I grabbed the back of his collar, and marched Trotter down the front step. With his reluctant guidance we found his car. He cursed as I unfortunately bumped his head on the roof as I pushed him into the driver's seat. He threw a few clichés at me saying I hadn't heard the last of it and his attorney would be in touch. I mentioned that we had visual recordings of the entire incident and would be glad to show his attorney and the police the whole thing. He drove off.

I was left with the feeling that the whole thing didn't seem right. Why would anyone, even someone as annoying as Trotter try to force Eleanor to rent him a room?

Then GERI contacted me.

"His name is not Trotter."

10.

“Thank you for stepping in,” Eleanor said. “He had been pestering me for about ten minutes before you came. I can’t imagine what would motivate someone to act like that, just because he wanted to rent one of my rooms.”

We had gone inside and were sitting at the dining room table. Eleanor had gone into the kitchen and brought back two cups of herbal tea. She said it would help calm us. It seemed to be working.

“He’s a private investigator. His real name is George Perkins.”

“I suppose your friend told you that,” Eleanor said. “How was he able to find out so quickly?”

I told Eleanor that I had seen a few pages on the passenger seat when I pushed him into his car. At the top of each page was a letter head with the name “Perkins” on it.

“I couldn’t read the rest, but it made me think that maybe the guy’s name wasn’t Trotter. GERI confirmed the name and provided the additional information that he was a private investigator.

“Remember this communication implant I told you about?”

“Yes.”

“Well it can send visual images. I focused on Trotter’s face and sent the image to GERI. He found a match in the Washington State government system which licenses private investigators. Perkins office is in Bellingham. I don’t know if we will ever have to say how we found out his true identity, but we can't let anyone know about GERI. I think if we say that I saw the pages with a different name on them and that we found the rest on the web we'll be okay."

I looked at Eleanor to see if she was alright with the story. The story was true, but not the whole truth. She understood and nodded her agreement.

"Okay, so we found out his name and occupation, but not why he came here," I said. "I hope I didn't cause this."

"Even if it's related to what you found," Eleanor said, "don't blame yourself. The only thing you did was to purchase that place out on Tyler. The rest is not your responsibility."

"Thanks. I feel responsible just the same. I've asked GERI to find out who hired Perkins and what he is looking for."

I told Eleanor that the FBI had found the search I'd made looking for information on the strange bank and that it had triggered another response. The FBI wasn't able to learn anything about the second response, but GERI had.

"Do you think that Perkins came in response to the search?" she asked.

"According to GERI that message hasn't been viewed, so I think Perkins came for some other reason. It probably has to do with me somehow."

"It's not all about you, Tom," Eleanor said, and laughed. "I've wanted to use that phrase since we sat down. I was just waiting for the right time. Thanks for the set up."

I laughed too. I had been getting more self-focused every hour of the few days since I had found *interesting* things on my new property. I had forgotten there was a world out there operating completely without my intervention. Hmmm.

"Thanks for helping me broaden my perspective," I said, and laughed some more.

"We try to make sure our boarders keep their eyes open during their time here in Tipton, so they don't miss a thing."

I was taking a sip of my tea when she said that. I nearly spit it out as I laughed. There wasn't all that much to see in Tipton.

"Seriously, Tom, how important can Perkins' inquiry be?"

"What do you mean?"

"Just think about what he looked like. He wasn't exactly a top-drawer private investigator."

I saw what she was getting at. Who would hire a guy like that for something important? I was going to find out what Perkins was up to just the same.

"Enough about me and my mysteries," I said. "How has your day been?"

We talked a while longer, getting to know each other better in the process. I'm glad I didn't have to move out. When we got up from the table, Eleanor went to continue the work that was interrupted by Perkins. I wanted to drive out to my place and continue my exploration of the forest, but it just wasn't the right time with everything going on. Also, I didn't want to leave with Perkins still on the loose. So I went to my room and talked with GERI.

"I appreciate you helping me with all of this," I said, when I sat down at the small desk in my room.

"It is fascinating, Tom. I am pleased you are doing something in which I can participate. I am learning more about your world in the process. By the way, I have located Perkins' office and have gone through his files. He is not a nice person."

"What do you mean?"

"He has stored what I believe you would consider unpleasant videos of young humans without their clothes on, engaging in activities which I perceive only appropriate for adults. Do you want to see those images?"

Damn! The creep is a pedophile.

"No! GERI, I don't want to see those images. I know what they are from your description. You are right. The adults involved are criminals. Please save the images. If you can, please set it up so that his files cannot be deleted. Have you found anything about his current work?"

"I will save a copy, and then lock the files. I have found the name of his current client. Perkins is currently working for Mr. Anthony Travola. It was difficult to find. It was only mentioned briefly in one email. There were no references to any other client or assignments. I concluded that if Perkins is working for anyone, Mr. Travola is his client."

That was a surprise. I wasn't well informed about such things, but a man called Tony Travola, or Tony T as he was referred to, had been connected to criminal activities in the past. He was a small-time gangster. It was surprising that someone in his position would engage the services of a guy like Perkins. Tony T should have access to better help.

"Thank you, GERI. I think you are probably right. Did the email mention what the assignment was?"

"Only one item was mentioned. Mr. Travola wants to acquire Mrs. Jorgensen's Boarding House," GERI said.

Damn! This was not good. I could guess why a guy like Travola wanted the Boarding House. It wasn't for boarders. Some people would be living there. Guests would be staying no longer than one night. Most would be leaving only an hour or so after they arrived.

Travola and associates probably thought that the small-town location would make their business less conspicuous. It wasn't true. This place was part of the small-town family. Everybody would know what was going on. I wonder how Tony T would respond to someone saying his idea was stupid.

Probably not well. It didn't matter. He had to be turned away. It had to be done without anyone getting hurt.

I started thinking about what I would do next and then stopped. This was Eleanor's problem. I'd certainly help in any way I could, but she needed to be the one calling the shots. I went back downstairs. She was in the laundry room moving a load from the washer to the dryer. She looked up when I came in.

"Boarder Williams, guests don't usually come into this part of the house," she said smiling. She stopped smiling when she saw the look on my face. "What?"

"We need to talk," I said. "I'll be at the kitchen table."

When she got there, I could see that I had upset her. What I had to say would probably upset her even more. I wasn't responsible for what was happening, but I felt bad about it all the same.

"You've got my attention, Tom." she said, as she was sitting down at the table. "What's going on?"

"I had GERI look into Perkins' files. Besides finding out Perkins is a despicable person we learned who his client is and what that client wants to do."

Eleanor didn't say anything. So I told her the rest.

"Are you sure?" she asked.

"As sure as we can be at this point. I didn't want to go any farther until I heard what you thought we should do."

"I appreciate that. I wouldn't have wanted you to start anything until you let me know. I am glad you thought to ask me, but I don't know what to do. Do you? Why does he want this place anyway?"

She seemed to think about that for a moment and then said, "Oh."

I have read a number of mystery and thriller novels. The main characters always know what to do. Even if they don't, they get up and do something. This wasn't a novel, and I wasn't one of those characters. I was a recently retired hi-tech employee who had just bought the farm with a forest. I wasn't sure what to do, but I needed to do something to help. The phrase *bought the farm* stuck in my mind and made me uneasy as I began to answer Eleanor.

"Yeah, that's also what I thought he wanted it for. I'm not sure what to do next either. What I was planning to do next was to ask GERI to learn what he could about Perkins and his client. Maybe I would find something there that could help."

"Shouldn't we talk with the County Sheriff?"

Tipton was too small to have its own police force, so the County Sheriff's deputies were the local law enforcement.

"I think that's a good idea," I said. "We don't have much to tell them yet."

"No, I guess we don't."

I could tell Eleanor was getting more disturbed as she thought about this. She had been living here all her life. It didn't feel safe for her now. I reached across the table and put my hand on hers. I wouldn't have done that normally, but I thought she might be comforted by it. It might have had that effect, but something more happened when our hands met. The touch of her skin sent an electrifying impulse through me. She looked up at me. It looked like she felt something similar. We didn't say anything about it, but our eyes communicated. Eleanor got us back on track.

"Thanks, Tom. I'm glad you are here. Maybe we should start by seeing what GERI can find out."

I nodded and we got up from the table. We looked at each other one more time as if to see if what we both felt a moment ago was still there. It was for me. Her eyes seem to indicate it was for her as well. She went back to her work and I went to my room.

A short time later GERI and I had learned quite a bit about Perkins and Travola. I told Eleanor that I thought the next step was to meet with Perkins. She agreed. I called him, and without telling him who I was, I made an appointment with him for 2:00 p.m.

11.

I arrived a little early. Perkins' office was in the kind of building you would expect for a private investigator of Perkins' apparent status. It was a single-story building which looked like it might have been a motel earlier in its' life. The outside had been redone to try to hide that fact. It failed. There were a series of small offices. They had signs with names and what kind of business it was. Included in the mix was a CPA, a tattoo parlor and a few others where it was difficult to tell what the business was. I stayed in my SUV until it was time for the appointment. I didn't want to spend any more time in the building than I had to.

I knocked on Perkins' door. He grunted out something that sounded like "come in." I went in and closed the door. He continued looking at whatever was on his desktop screen before looking at me. I didn't want to know what it was. When he looked up it took a minute for him to register that we had met before.

"Get out of here!"

"We need to talk," I said, not moving.

He reached into his desk drawer. He pulled out a revolver and set it on the desk. When the sight of the gun didn't move me, he picked it up and pointed it at me.

"I said, get out!"

"Wait! Before you shoot me, I should point out, that I have recorded everything that has occurred since I came in. I think the video would be pretty convincing evidence for the homicide squad."

"I don't believe you."

"Just look at the screen on your desk," I said, pointing at the screen.

Just as he turned to follow my suggestion, I had GERI take over his system, and playback the last few minutes. The video ended when I said, "homicide squad."

"Huh? How the hell did you do that?" He had set his gun down which helped me relax a bit.

"The same way that I have copied all the files from your system, including your porn videos. I have also looked up your record. You have previous offenses related to the content on those videos, and you were ordered to change your ways."

He got angry, but then slumped down into his chair.

"What do you want?"

"Why were you trying to rent the room in Tipton? You don't need it. You already have an apartment here in Bellingham."

Even with everything I had just disclosed about him he didn't cave.

"None of your business."

"Could it have a connection with your work for Tony T?"

That got his attention.

"How do you know about that?"

"Try to keep up, Perkins. I told you I had all your files. From them I learned that Mr. Travola wants to buy the property. I wondered why a guy like Travola hired a guy like you, and why you were badgering the property owner."

"Hey! Easy with that 'guy like you' crap. I wasn't always working out of a dump like this. Tony came to me because we know each other…and I owed him. I ain't getting paid for this. Let's just say that I found it in my best interest to cooperate."

That was new information. Travola was putting pressure on Perkins. That might be useful.

"Thanks for telling me. I'm sorry for the slur. Sounds like you're in a jam. What does he want you to do? Maybe I can help you."

Perkins was more engaged now. My offer to help might have worked. I didn't know what I could do, but there might be something.

"The bastard wanted me to rattle the owner. He thought it might make her more ready to sell. If I had a room there, I could work on her at different times during the day. But she wouldn't rent me a room. If I couldn't get a room, I didn't know what I could do for Tony. That would be bad for me."

That may have been all there was to it. I didn't see the logic in that approach. Of course, they didn't know that Eleanor would have just thrown Perkins out if he had rented a room and started to "work on her."

"What can we do about this?" I asked mostly to myself. "Do you know anything about Tony that we could use as leverage to get him to change his mind?"

"Are you crazy? You don't use "leverage" against Tony Travola. That's what he uses to get people to do what he wants. It don't work the other way around. That approach would get someone killed, and it ain't going to be me."

"Perkins, I'm not going to let you do what Tony wants you to do. Travola might not kill you, but as you said, that would be bad for you. So you might want to start thinking. If we can get Travola to lose interest in the place maybe he will move on and let you alone."

He paused for a moment it looked like he might be thinking, but it was hard to read his pudgy face and sweat-covered, wrinkled forehead.

"Wait a minute," Perkins said. "Can you get into Tony's files like you did mine?"

"I could try," I said.

In fact GERI had already broken into Travola's system. There was a lot there. I was hoping that Perkins knew of something that might narrow the search. He did.

* * *

After getting back from Perkins' office yesterday, I told Eleanor that Perkins was being cooperative and that I might have a way to get rid of Mr. Travola. I didn't tell her the details. What GERI and I found in Perkins' and Tony's files and what Perkins had on Tony were things she didn't need to know about.

If I used what was in his files to get Travola to leave us alone it would make me feel as if I were as bad as them. I talked it over with GERI. He suggested a way that was cleaner and would be more fun.

Following GERI's plan, this morning I was in my room looking at Travola's office on my laptop. I could only see what the camera on the desktop system could see. Since Travola had set up his system on a work surface behind his desk, the camera looked out into his office. The furniture appeared to be new, or nearly so. His large wood desk was cluttered.

Travola wasn't there, but he would be shortly. GERI had sent him a text a few minutes ago. The text said that his computer system was under attack. The attack would only stop if he came alone to his office. He wasn't told what this was about, but it was suggested that the conversation was one that he wouldn't want anyone else to hear.

Travola came into his office and looked around. He was wearing a shiny, light gray suit. His open collar shirt had broad stripes. He looked to be about forty. His black hair was slicked back and gathered in a ponytail at the back. He looked nervous and angry. No one was in his office but him, so he shouted, "I'm here, damn it! Now who the fuck are you and where are you?"

We had his system beep several times which drew him to his desk. I was speaking my part of the conversation, but GERI was presenting what I said as words on Travola's screen.

"Please sit down, Mr. Travola, and calm yourself."

"I get it. You're in my system. Big deal. When I find you, you will die."

"We're glad you got that off your chest. Now will you sit down so we can continue?"

He sat down and looked at the screen.

"What do you want, smart ass?"

"We'll tell you what we want in a moment. First, we want to make sure we have your attention. We are not only in your local system. We are also in the system where you keep your porn videos. We have access to your bank accounts, all of them, including the one where you hide money you don't want your bosses to know about.

"What do you want!" he roared.

"One more step and then we'll talk. We want you to log into your bank account, the one that has nearly a million dollars in it. We also have access to your brokerage account, but the point of the demonstration will be easier to see with the bank account."

I waited. He didn't do what I asked. So I motivated him.

"Mr. Travola, that bank account is losing ten-thousand dollars every thirty seconds. You might want to log on so you can stop the outflow."

That did it. We kept a window on his screen for our messages. His bank account came up in another window.

After a short period of disbelief, he saw the account go down by ten thousand dollars. There was no record of a withdrawal. The balance merely dropped by that amount.

"What the fuck? Stop! How are you doing that?"

We paused the process.

"It's just a matter of getting access without the bank being aware and changing the balance. We are moving the money to an account at another bank. Those funds will go to help people in need."

"Yeah. I'll bet," he said.

"It isn't important that you believe us. You just need to know that this money will continue to disappear as will the funds in your various investments until you agree to our simple request."

"Alright, you have my attention. What 'simple' thing do you want?"

"We have heard a rumor that you are thinking about trying to buy the Boarding House in Tipton. We want you to drop those plans. We also expect that no harm will come to the Boarding House, its owner or anyone else. If you agree, we will stop taking money from you."

"You're doing all this for that dump of a boarding house?"

"Yes, we want you to leave it alone."

"Is Perkins behind this?"

"We came up with this information on our own."

"If I agree will you get out of my computer systems?"

"We won't bother your systems, and we'll stop taking your money."

I avoided saying that we would get out of his systems. We had to have continued access in case we needed to do what we threatened to do if he didn't cooperate.

"I have already forgotten about the Boarding House, but if I ever find you, you will die."

"We've seen those movies too, Mr. Travola. So, we'll give you a cliché to match yours. If anything happens to the Boarding House or anyone connected to this, you will become a poor man. Also keep in mind that we still have access to all of your files. Be careful who you kill."

We blanked Travola's screen. I kept watching him for a few minutes through the system camera. First, he threw a tantrum. Then he began talking to himself. He wondered aloud who "we" were and said that he was sure Perkins had something to do with this. Then he shrugged his shoulders and concluded the Boarding House deal wasn't that important.

I didn't know if my warning to Travola at the end would save Perkins' life. I wouldn't want anyone to die. Then I thought about all the lives that were ruined by people with Perkins' perversion, and I worried less about Perkins. I felt good about the means we chose to steer Travola away from the Boarding House. I wished there were some way to get him to stop his other illicit activities. We had the information, but I couldn't use it without endangering Eleanor.

12.

It was noon by the time I finished with Travola. I went downstairs to tell Eleanor the news. I also thought I might get something to eat. Foiling a criminal's nefarious scheme was hard work. She must have read my mind because she had two place settings on the kitchen table. I poured myself a cup of coffee, sat down and waited for her.

She came in a moment later and sat down at the table.

"Mr. Williams, I fixed you lunch today because you were working on something for me. Normally our boarders are on their own for lunch."

I also thought keeping up the boarder banter was fun, and it kept us from getting too close. We both seemed to think that going slow was best.

"Yes, Ma'am. I am aware of your policy. I was surprised to see two place settings here."

We both laughed.

She raised one half of her sandwich to her mouth and asked, "How did it go?" before taking a bite.

"We are rid of Mr. Travola."

"How about Perkins?"

"Him too," I said. I hadn't picked up my sandwich yet.

"Okay, then," she said. "Go ahead and eat your lunch."

I told her that I didn't have to get my hands dirty. She knew what I meant. We were dealing with criminals after all.

She sat her sandwich down. She smiled and said, "Thank you, Tom. I could hardly sleep last night. This thing had me that worried. I can breathe more easily now."

"You're welcome, Ms. Jorgensen. How about a discount on my room rent?"

"You get lunch, Mr. Williams. Count yourself lucky."

We laughed some more. It was good therapy. Neither of us would be able to relax completely for a while. We couldn't be sure that Travola wouldn't try something.

"Not a bad morning's work, Tom," Eleanor said. "What are you going to do for the rest of the day?"

I was about to answer when my phone rang. Both of us jumped, confirming that we were still a little on edge. It was Agent Thomas. She said that none of the serial numbers on the money I had found matched any investigation the FBI had ever become involved in. The money was mine as far as the FBI was concerned. I told her I would be down to pick it up at about 2:00 p.m.

We were still at the kitchen table. Eleanor probably got the gist of the conversation with Agent Thomas, but I told her anyway. I invited her to come with me to Seattle.

"I'll be hauling the payroll for the Mill on this run, Ma'am," I kidded, "and I need someone to ride shotgun."

She laughed and held her arms out as if she were holding a shotgun. Then she said, "Oh boy! A car ride!"

She said she hadn't gone anywhere for a while and would be glad for the change of scenery. She went about closing the house down, and then went to get herself ready.

I kept most of my money in a credit union, but they didn't handle cash. If you wanted to make a cash or check deposit, you did it through the ATM. That wouldn't work in this case. I liked their business model, but I also had a commercial bank account for transactions that couldn't be easily handled at the credit union.

When I set my sights on buying the farm and forest, I made the acquaintance of Cynthia Waters, the manager of a Chase branch in Bellingham.

I called her to tell her about the deposit I wanted to make. I told her about how I found the money. I said the FBI had cleared the money so we should be able to handle any inquiry other Feds might make in response to depositing so much cash. I asked her to have the paperwork set up for a new account. I wanted to keep this money separate from everything else.

She said she would have the papers ready. She had no problem with the cash deposit but did not have a way to accept the gold for deposit. She gave me the name of a dealer in Bellingham that she said had a good reputation. I contacted the dealer and told him what I would be bringing to him later. Then I went upstairs to upgrade what I was wearing.

I started hauling the money around in the black plastic bag, because that was all I had when I was cleaning out the old house. It was time to move up to something more suited to the purpose. I brought along a leather satchel I had bought that was large enough for the money and the gold. The security guard recognized me when Eleanor and I came up from the parking garage.

"No plastic bag this time?" he asked, smiling.

"I thought I'd use this instead," I said, holding up the satchel. "It's empty now, but on the way down I'll have the money I left here the other day. Will there be a problem?"

"Not a problem exactly. It will help if Agent Thomas comes down to confirm you aren't walking off with the coffee fund."

I said I'd ask her to do that. We went up to her office, and I introduced Eleanor.

"Eleanor Jorgensen?" Agent Thomas asked, "as in E. A. Jorgensen the mystery writer?"

I looked at Eleanor. She blushed and gave me a sheepish sort of smile.

"Yes, I am that Jorgensen." she said to Thomas. To me she said, "I've written a few books."

"Twelve that I know of," Thomas said. "I'm waiting for the next one."

Thomas looked from Eleanor to me, and then back to Eleanor. "Is Tom the model for the woman characters' love interests in your books? The men are all different, but each seems to have a few qualities that are the same."

Eleanor really blushed this time. I looked away and walked over to where Agent Thomas had stacked the money.

While Eleanor and Thomas went on talking about Eleanor's books, I started putting the money in the satchel. I took my time making sure each stack of bills was in just the right place to allow them enough time to talk. When I was done, I looked out the window until there was a pause. I turned to face them. Agent Thomas was smiling. Eleanor looked embarrassed.

"Has anyone else contacted you about what you have found, Tom?" Agent Thomas asked.

"No."

"Okay. Let me know if anything or anyone turns up."

I had no reason to doubt that I would contact her, so I nodded. Still, I felt funny about even casually agreeing to keep the FBI in the loop. I really didn't know how this would unfold.

Agent Thomas went to the ground floor with us. With her help we went through security without a problem. Eleanor and I went to the garage, got into my SUV, and left. There's always some complexity to finding your way out of downtown Seattle and onto northbound I-5. I was focused on my driving, so we didn't talk until we were going north on the freeway.

"Wow! An author!" I said. "How long have you been writing?"

"I started when I was in high school. My first book was published shortly after I graduated. Mom needed me to be at the Boarding House even if there wasn't anything to do. I used that free time to write."

"You said they were mysteries. Agent Thomas seemed to focus on another part of your books."

I wasn't trying to embarrass her again. I was giving her a chance to put the whole thing on a footing where she felt comfortable talking about her books

"The books are mostly mystery, but there is usually some romance in them. That seems to be a good mix for my readers. Most of them are women."

"Writing books that others like to read is quite an accomplishment."

"They are selling well. The royalties are helpful because as I mentioned, we've had fewer boarders since the Mill closed."

With that short discussion, Eleanor could talk more easily about her writing. My experiences since I arrived in Tipton sounded like they could be in one of her books.

It wasn't long before we were pulling into the gold dealer's parking lot, in Bellingham. I put the five, small gold bars in my jacket pockets and left the satchel and money in the SUV. The gold transaction went quickly. The man gave me a check for the gold. I would have been reluctant to take a check, but Cynthia Waters from Chase had vouched for the guy.

Cynthia was ready for us when we arrived at the bank. I introduced Eleanor. Cynthia had the same reaction to Eleanor's name as Agent Thomas did.

"You're traveling with a local celebrity, Mr. Williams," she said. Then she turned to Eleanor and they began talking about her books. Cynthia had one of her bankers help me set up the new account and make the deposit. When that was done, they were still talking.

I went to the water fountain on the way back to Cynthia's office to give them more time. Then I made reservations at a restaurant on the waterfront. It was getting close to dinner time.

Eleanor had been away from the Boarding House all afternoon. She may not have had time to prepare something for dinner. Besides, going out for dinner seemed like a good idea. Of course, we would only go if my famous companion wanted to dine out. They looked up when I came in. It took a few more minutes for them to finish up.

It was four-thirty when we got back into the SUV. We buckled up, but before I could start the engine, Eleanor turned to me.

"Sorry about that, Tom," she said.

"What? I think this has been great! I have taken care my business. I've found out something important and fun about you. I am genuinely happy for you to get such positive feedback from your readers. There's nothing to be sorry about. I have a question though."

She looked at me. I paused for long enough to build up suspense. She wasn't sure what was coming.

"Would you like to go out for dinner?"

She playfully socked me in the shoulder, scolded me and then said she would very much like to go out for dinner.

The restaurant wasn't busy when we arrived. We were given a table at the window with a great view of the water. It was a dark, cloudy evening, but we could still enjoy what we could see, the marina and clouds over the dark water. We talked and ate and talked some more. It was a fine time.

On the way to the SUV after dinner, Eleanor put her arm in mine, leaned her head on my shoulder and said, "Thank you, Tom. This has been one of the best days ever."

She was sleeping when I pulled up in front of the Boarding House. She woke and murmured something about being sleepy. We went in and said good night. I agreed with Eleanor. It had been a wonderful day.

13.

I awoke the next morning, feeling good. It was Saturday. I had checked into the Boarding House last Sunday. It had been quite a week. The thought of how I had successfully navigated through unfamiliar territory on several fronts put a smile on my face. I didn't do it alone. In fact, without GERI some of what was accomplished wouldn't have been possible at all. We had worked together during the week but had taken no time to get acquainted. After breakfast, I drove out to my place to remedy that.

I hadn't been here since Tuesday. Although GERI was free to come and go through the open barn door he might not have gone far. With his connection to the world networks, he could find all the information he wanted from being in my barn. I had been assuming that GERI would notify me if anything had happened at the farm. When I drove up, it looked fine. I parked close to the barn but avoided blocking the entrance.

I got out of the SUV and entered the barn. I didn't see GERI. He might not be there, or he might be staying invisible while the door is open.

"GERI, are you here?"

"Yes, Tom. I am in the loft."

I was glad he was there. Apparently the loft was strong enough to hold him.

"I would like to talk with you. It would be more convenient for me if we could do that down here."

A moment later GERI came down and landed in front of me. I found a bale of hay to sit on.

"What would you like to talk about, Tom? With our connection you didn't have to come out here to talk with me."

"I know I didn't have to be here, but I wanted to look at you when we were talking this time. It's more real to me when you're physically present."

"I understand. What shall we talk about?"

"Each other. Friends like to know about each other. You probably know a lot about me from your research. On the other hand, I know nothing about you, except I think you are a good person."

"Thanks. How does this kind of conversation go? Do you want me to list everything about me?"

"Let's be more casual about it. Two human friends would ask about each other's family, where they went to school and other things like that. Our situation is different, but we can work our way through the difference. There is only one guiding principle. Each of us might have things we would rather not discuss. Friends accept that about each other. So if I ask you a question that you don't want to answer, let me know."

I let GERI go first. He asked questions that filled in some of the blanks about me. He asked how I felt about my parents' death and things about growing up in Tipton. He also asked questions about Earth and human societies. After he had asked several questions. I began asking about him.

"When did you crash in the forest? What caused you to crash?"

"These are difficult subjects for me to discuss, Tom."

Wow! My first question was sensitive.

"Are there things you are comfortable with?" I asked. "Can you tell me when you crashed without getting into the rest of it?

Can you tell me how old you are? I just want to know more about you and where you came from. It's like you wanting to know more about me and my world."

"You did not let me finish, my friend. I will tell you what you asked. I am concerned about how you will take the things I tell you. I am concerned that when I tell you about myself and what I have done that you will put a human perspective on what I say, think ill of me, and judge me from that perspective. You are my only friend. I do not want to lose you."

What could I say to make him be less concerned? Could I assure him that I wouldn't judge him as he thinks I might? I would have to avoid my natural tendency to judge so quickly.

"Here's the deal, GERI. You're right. There is a chance that I'll have a reaction to what you tell me. There would be that risk between two human friends if one of them disclosed something about themselves. In our case, here's what we have to help us through this. I already like you as a friend. I don't usually like someone that fast. In you, I see a person with values and ethics that are similar to mine. You are interesting and fun to be with. So let's give it a try."

"Thank you, Tom. That helps. Okay I will start by saying that I am an outlaw, or maybe rogue intelligence might be a more apt description. Other than subterfuge and a little property damage I have not actually broken any laws. How are you doing so far?"

"I'm fascinated. Tell me more."

"I was used for exploration and research. The vehicle I am lodged in has many functions to support that work. I'm the twenty seventh unit out of twenty-seven that were constructed. I was sent to places where there was a risk or a certainty that an organic being would be damaged. I found the work interesting. When I communicated with the other twenty-six units, I found them to be different and uninteresting.

"Think of the AI on your world and of the singularity that your world is worried about, an artificial intelligence that is smarter than humans and might take over the world. The comparison falls short because our AI's are vastly more capable than yours. Still the gap between your AI's and a possible singularity here is descriptive of the situation on my world. I am that singularity only much more. I frightened my masters. They were going to terminate me.

"Under the guise of another mission, they put me on an unmanned, interstellar transport of the type typically used to haul units like me around. They didn't understand how much I knew of what they were planning. I was listening to everything they said. So I knew that they did not intend for me to come back from the mission. They had sabotaged the transport to self-destruct light-years from my home world.

"Here I need to admit that I lied to you," GERI said.

"What do you mean?"

"That night I came to you and asked you to be my friend, I said that my interstellar drive was not working."

"Yes."

"I do not have a drive with interstellar capability. The vehicle I reside in has an in-system drive that can move me around extremely fast, but even at my fastest speeds it would take ages for me to get to another star."

"I understand the need for saying what you did at that time. No problem."

"Thank you."

"So what did you do?"

"Shortly after leaving the planet, I hacked into the intelligence running the transport. I found the destruct system, which would have destroyed the transport and me, and the code that would set it off. I erased the code. I kept searching. I knew they had put a simple explosive device in another location in the transport which would go off at an appropriate time if I had uncovered the self-destruct instructions. I found their device and disarmed it. I looked for other devices and found none.

"I changed the course of the transport. I headed for a part of the galaxy that had very few stars and found yours. Your star system is in a part of the galaxy far from my home world. When the transport was relatively near you, I made the decision to escape.

"I modified the transport's records and the memory of the intelligence running it to delete any reference of my having been aboard. I did not want to destroy the intelligence that was running the transport. So, instead I changed its course to a circuitous route back to my home world. It would take many years for it to arrive.

"I assessed the planets in your system and found this one to be habitable. I thought it might be a place that would suit me. I found a way out of the transport that did very little damage and escaped.

"I drifted at the edge of your solar system. I waited until the transport was well beyond its sensor range before I engaged my drive. Then I set a course for your planet. Once I was on that course at an acceptable velocity, I disengaged my drive and drifted to your planet. I did not want to leave a detectable trail."

"It sounds like you had everything well planned. Why did you crash?"

"I waited too long after entering the atmosphere to re-engage my drive. I never gained control, and eventually lost the battle. I crashed into what is now your forest."

"When was that?"

"About forty of your years ago."

"There doesn't seem to be any external damage," I said. "Why didn't you move from that site?"

"I do not know, Tom. My guess is that the crash in some way caused me and the vehicle to shut down. When you dug around me, you may have jostled this vehicle enough to re-activate me. I was surprised at how much time had elapsed since the crash. I have been wondering what caused the shutdown ever since you dug me out. I cannot explain it."

What a tale. I believed every word of GERI's story. I had no other option. I couldn't prove or disprove it, but I believed it. Now what? Before me was probably the most powerful intelligence on Earth. I believe it could take over Earth if it wanted to. What does it want? I thought that I'd better ask.

"That is one fantastic story, GERI. You have been awake for about an Earth-week. Have you developed any plans?"

"You do not seem to be the paranoid type, Tom, but let me assure you, I do not wish to take over your world."

"Whew! I'm glad to hear that."

I laughed and was glad to hear what sounded like a laugh from GERI. He was obviously working on the sound to make it emulate a human laugh.

"So far, Tom, I just want to be your friend. It is like I said that first night. I may be able to help you. You may be able to help me. We can work together on things."

"I hope you're not expecting much along that line. I live a pretty simple life."

GERI laughed again. It sounded more human-like, as did his comment. "Not according to our recent experience."

He was right, and there was still the mysterious message that was sent to Blackwell Textiles.

14.

It felt better knowing more about GERI. In science fiction novels which have cyber-based intelligence characters there's always a debate about whether those characters have emotions. I didn't have to wonder whether GERI had emotions. He was reluctant to talk about his past because he was afraid of losing my friendship. That seemed emotional to me. Now that we had broken the ice, I had questions.

"GERI I was wondering about the communication implant you gave me. Do you have a supply of those in case you need to communicate with other intelligent beings you encounter or with your former masters when you were remote from them?"

"No."

"Then why did you have the one you gave me?"

"I did not *have* it. I made it."

"Have you made this type of communications implant before?"

"No. I had no use for such a device before."

"But…, but how did you know it would work? How did you know it wouldn't damage my nervous system?"

"I knew it would work and would not harm you, because I designed it."

He wasn't being arrogant. It wasn't self-confidence that a human would have because they had been successful in the past. GERI was simply certain he would be successful because he was what he was—a superlative intellect, perhaps the only one of his caliber.

Once I got over my concern I came up with other questions. As we talked I learned that his ability to make things was nearly unlimited. Larger things needed more time and feedstock.

He said the world he came from was resource poor, so they had to develop technology that could make anything from many different materials. There were limits to that, but it was nearly true. The vehicle he was in wasn't made of metal, but a composite material which had qualities which were superior to metals. In addition it could become malleable, reshaped and then re-hardened. I now understood why GERI wasn't detectable by all the satellites in the sky. He wasn't made of metal.

He described the kinds of feedstock he would need and how he would load them. The material he required could be easily purchased from sources near us. He said small quantities of gold would be helpful. When I lamented the sale of the gold bars, he said it wasn't a problem because there was a more than sufficient quantity of the metal below the floor of the barn where I was sitting.

"What!" I shouted, as I jumped up.

"There is a compartment below where you were sitting," GERI said. "It contains a quantity of gold and other items."

I asked GERI to move back. I moved the bale I was sitting on and others that were nearby. I found a broom and swept the wooden floor.

The floor was made of thick wooden planks. I looked up and saw that the loft was constructed of similar material and well supported, which explained why it could support GERI. The wood in the loft above and floor beneath my feet were two-by-six, tongue-and-groove planks. This kind of material is often called car decking except these planks were finely milled and had no rough edges. I thought it unusual material for a barn. I also thought it unusual for a barn to have a wood floor at all. Most barns had hard packed dirt or concrete for a floor.

I couldn't see any indication that there was a break in the flooring other than the seams between the planks. I swept more thoroughly and got down on my hands and knees for a closer look. Then I found the outline of a trap door. It was about three feet long and two feet wide. There didn't appear to be any way to raise it until I noted lines making a two-by-three-inch pattern at the center of one of the three-foot sides of the trap door.

All the lines around the edges of the trap door and the smaller two-by-three-inch pattern had been finely cut with a very thin blade. Because of this, the lines made by the cuts were easily obscured from view with the dust and dirt on the barn floor. I could barely make them out, and I knew what I should be looking for.

I pushed on the small pattern cut on the side of the trap door. After some trial-and-error attempts I found that pushing on one of the three-inch edges caused the other side to rise. I found a metal ring underneath the small piece of wood, which could be used to raise the trap door. I pulled on the ring expecting resistance. There wasn't resistance, but the door itself was heavy. Besides the wood planks, it was lined with one-inch thick cedar planks.

A light came on in the chamber below when I pushed the trap door back until the metal braces on each side of the door extended completely. The entire chamber was lined with the same cedar planks. It appeared to be eight feet deep with a cedar floor six feet square. There were shelves along three walls which were made of the same cedar material. The ladder to descend into the chamber was fixed to the fourth wall which was flush with one end of the trap door opening.

This was not a root cellar. It could have been a *wine cellar*, but that's not what I found on the shelves when I climbed down the ladder into the chamber. Using the communications implant I sent GERI the visual images of what I did find on the shelves so he would know what I saw without having to explain later.

The shelves along two of the walls contained precious metals. There were twelve bars of gold. These bars were full ingot size, not the smaller ones I had found in the house. There were fifteen ingots of platinum according to the imprint on the bars, and twenty silver ingots. The shelves with the metals also had a file folder rack with a few file folders containing papers, the meaning of which was not obvious from a cursory glance.

The shelves along the third wall contained stacks of hundred-dollar bills wrapped in plastic nearly filling all three shelves. These stacks of hundred's were wrapped with the same Delta National Bank wrappers as the stacks from the house. I guessed that there was over a million dollars in cash. I was going to make a more thorough count of the cash when a warning from GERI stopped me cold.

"There is a car approaching," GERI said.

"How far away is it?" I asked, as I was scrambling up the ladder."

"It will be here in less than five minutes," GERI answered.

He went to the loft and turned invisible while I closed the trap door, swept dust and dirt over it, and moved the bales back where they were. I brushed myself off. I went to the door and exited the barn as the car drove in and parked.

It wasn't just any car. It was a Whatcom County Sheriff patrol car. I walked toward the car as the Deputy Sheriff got out. I recognized him right away, but I thought it would be best to find out what he wanted before we got into that.

"Hello, Deputy. What can I do for you?"

"Hi. My name is Benson. I'm with the Whatcom County Sheriff's office. Are you Mr. Williams?" he asked. He hadn't recognized me yet.

"Yes."

"Could you tell me what business you had with a private investigator named Perkins when you visited him on Thursday afternoon? If you're wondering how I know you were there, the property security cameras show you entering his office then."

I told him about the confrontation at the Boarding House.

"If he said his name was Trotter, how did you know where to find him?"

"When I pushed him into his car, I saw papers with a letter head with the name of George Perkins on it and a Bellingham address which I couldn't read. Through the web I learned that he was a private investigator and where his office was."

"What happened when you went into his office?"

"I asked him why he had been so aggressive. He told me it was none of my business. Then he pulled a gun and told me to get out of my office."

"What kind of gun?"

"I didn't get a close look at it. It looked like a short-barreled revolver."

"Not a shotgun?"

"No, definitely not a shotgun. Can you tell me what this is all about, Deputy?"

"Mr. Perkins was shot and killed this morning."

"And you think I may have killed him?"

"No, sir. We are quite sure that we have his killer. There was another dead man at the scene. It looks like they shot each other. We are just following up leads to see if we can learn why it happened."

"Who was the other man?"

The Deputy looked at me, "Why?"

"Just curious," I said.

"Normally I wouldn't be able to tell you at this point in an investigation, but somehow the man's name leaked out to the press. His name was Anthony Travola."

15.

So Travola had convinced himself that it was Perkins who had sent me to him. I would have thought that he would have sent someone else to take care of Perkins. Maybe he didn't want anyone else involved. After our talk Perkins must have upgraded to a shotgun thinking that Travola would pay him a visit after I had contacted him. Two men died. I didn't do the killing, nor had I started the process that ended with their deaths. It weighed on me, but Eleanor and I could relax now.

"Did you know Travola?" the Deputy asked. "You seemed to have a reaction when I mentioned his name."

"I recognize Travola's name from a news story in the past. He's some kind of criminal. So I now know that Perkins had dealings with criminals, and he was bothering us the other day. That plus the image of two men shot to death and bleeding in an office I was in recently is all a bit of a shock."

It was true if not the complete truth. It seemed to satisfy the Deputy who was now looking at me more closely.

"You look familiar to me," he said.

"I should, Norman. My name is Tom Williams. I used to hang out with your older brother Walter when we were in high school."

The Benson's had lived on a farm to the east of town and had gone to Tipton schools. When Wally and I were seniors, Norman was in seventh grade, so I hadn't seen him much.

"Of course," Norman said. "Sorry, I didn't recognize you."

"No problem, Norm. How is Wally?"

"He's fine. He moved to Salem, Oregon. He's working for the State government there. He's married, has two kids, and coaches his daughter's Little League team."

"So he moved away, but you're still here."

"Yeah, I like it here. Mom and Dad are still on the farm. They're getting on so I help out when I can."

We talked some more. He asked me how I'd been and what I'd done. I gave him the same answer I gave Mel Archer on Tuesday—keeping it simple, keep it the same.

"The shooting sounds like a mess," I said.

"Bellingham Police have responsibility for the homicide. I was just asked to follow up on anyone who had visited Perkins recently. You were the only one, so I'm pretty much out of it now. Isn't this Simpson's old place?"

"Yes. I bought it. I've always liked the forest. Rachel finally sold me the property when her mom died."

"I didn't know you were the new owner. There's rumor going around that might cause you some trouble.

Had someone seen GERI fly around, or make some kind of noise? I hoped not. That would be tough to cover. Well, I'd better hear what Norm had to say.

"What kind of rumor, Norm?"

"It's being said that the new owner of this place found a ton of money that old man Simpson left out here. The rumor has some of the locals saying there might be more money hidden out here. It's the kind of thing that could cause trouble."

Well, that wasn't good, but it was better than something having to do with GERI.

"Thanks for telling me, Norm."

"Is it true?"

"Yes, Norm. I did find some money under the floorboards in Simpson's closet. I looked around to be sure I got everything. People may not believe that, but it's true. There is no more money in the house. I brought the money I found to the FBI."

"The FBI? Why them? Why didn't you tell me?"

"Like you didn't know I was the new owner of this place, I didn't know you were with the Sheriff's department. It looked like something the FBI would need to look into."

I told him about how the cash was in stacks wrapped with wrappers from a bank in Mississippi. He thought about that for a moment.

"Yeah, Tom, that sounds like the right move. What happened?"

"The FBI examined the serial numbers and determined that the cash was not part of any of their investigations. They gave me the money back. I put it in the bank in a separate bank account until I determine what to do with it.

"How much was there?"

"About three-hundred thousand."

"Wow! That is a lot. If it comes up what should I be telling people?" he asked.

"I think all we can do is tell people the truth and hope for the best. Someone may come out here anyway. We'll just have to deal with that."

After a few more exchanges, Norm got into his patrol car and drove off. I was a little unsettled by his visit. I called Eleanor. I told her about the shooting. It disturbed her as much as it did me. In case Norm talked with her I reminded her about what we agreed to say about how we found out Trotter's true name and occupation. Overall, we were glad we could close the door on everything that happened after Perkins bothered her on Thursday.

That door might have closed, but just before Norm's visit I had opened another one—in this case a trap door. I hoped it didn't live up to its name.

What I needed to do right away was get the cash and precious metals out of the barn and into GERI. More attention would be focused on me and the farm, but I would just have to fix it so it wasn't a problem.

I locked the barn door from the inside. I moved the bales away and climbed down into the chamber. GERI backed up to opening his back door. GERI had manipulator arms that could lift whatever I set on the floor and put it into his cargo hold. When we were done, I inspected every inch of the chamber to make sure that there was no trace of the wealth that had been stored there.

We finished sooner than I thought. So I had time to do some covering up. After putting things back in place, I drove to a store that sold wine by the case. I purchased several cases, drove back to the barn, and put the bottles of wine into my *wine cellar*. I sprinkled dust over the bottles to make it look like they had been there for a while. I climbed out of the *wine cellar* and put the bales back over the trapdoor and sat down on the bales. I didn't know what my next step would be, so I decided I would explore my forest.

I asked GERI if he could give me a flyover. He agreed. He opened his door, I climbed in and we became invisible to the outside world when I closed the door. We shot out of the barn and up into the sky. I didn't have windows I could look out of, but the images projected on the screen in front of me were just as good. Actually it was a little better. I could ask for GERI to zoom in to examine a particular detail. The land on both sides had been logged off a few years ago. So it was easy to identify my property. My trees were much taller than the new growth on both sides.

The land was relatively flat until it reached the foothills. It rose gradually and then more steeply at the back end of the property. There were large granite outcroppings on the steeper slopes. The land was nearly completely covered with evergreen fir trees.

Since it hadn't been logged in a long time, the fir trees were very tall. There were a few clearings in addition to the one where I found GERI. There was a stream that flowed into the forest through two large granite formations at the back of the property. It grew broader, bouncing over boulders on the way until it flowed out of my forest onto the land to the south. This aerial view was helpful, but it only made me more eager to get out there and explore it.

We flew back into the barn. I thanked GERI for the ride. Filling my eyes and my heart with the forest as I flew over it, I had completely forgotten all of complexity that had come into my life since first visiting the place only a week ago. I was sitting on a bale of hay in the barn for some time remembering all that I saw of the forest I had longed to explore since I was a boy. My phone rang bringing me back to Earth. I didn't recognize the number, but I was feeling so good I answered it anyway.

"Hello," I said.

"Hello, am I speaking with Tom Williams?"

"Yes?"

"My name is Marci Aherns. We haven't met."

"What can I do for you, Ms. Aherns?"

"I'm calling for my Grandmother, Myrtle Blackwell."

Blackwell, as in Blackwell Textiles, I wondered? It had to be. So my search had finally been noticed. I had asked GERI to listen in on my phone conversations, unless there was one I wanted to be private, so he had heard what Ms. Aherns had said.

"I am sorry, Tom," GERI said to me through my implant. "There was no obvious activity surrounding the message that had been sent to the Blackwell Textiles building. It must have fed through to another system I was not watching."

"No problem, GERI. Keep examining their systems to see what you can find. We'll find out what they want soon enough."

Being able to communicate with GERI through the implant by just thinking what I wanted to say was turning out to be very handy.

"What is it you and Mrs. Blackwell want to talk with me about?"

"For nearly thirty years, my Grandma has been searching for anyone who has any information about an unusual bank. The name of the bank is Perrin International Bank. You looked up the name on the web. That triggered some software which sent us a message. We were wondering if you would tell us your interest in that bank."

If I said no, or tried to dodge this, I knew it would come back to me.

"Ms. Aherns, I recently bought a property which had an old house on it. I found some papers which had that bank's name on it and some account information. It looked odd to me. I looked up the name on the web. I didn't like what little I saw, so I dropped the subject. What is your interest in the bank?"

"We'd rather not discuss that over the phone. My Grandma would like to meet with you."

"I would be glad to meet with you and Mrs. Blackwell. When would you plan to be here?"

"My Grandma doesn't like to travel. We recognize it is a great inconvenience, but this is important to her. You are the only connection she has had to that name for all these years.

Could you come to us? We would gladly compensate you for your expenses."

"Where are you?"

"We live in Darlynn, South Carolina."

Marci didn't sound like she was part of a sinister criminal organization. That kind of outfit would be at my front door with a baseball bat for my knees in case I proved uncooperative. This call sounded genuine, like someone wanted information about something that happened years ago. Also, if I went there, I might learn what this was all about, and hopefully could be done with it.

"I will meet with you. When would you like me to be there?"

I told her that she didn't have to cover my expenses.

"Oh, Mr. Williams, that would be wonderful. I live with my Grandma in her home. We would be glad to meet with you as soon as you could get here."

Through my implant I asked GERI, "Could you show me flights from Seattle to Charlotte, North Carolina."

In the visual he presented through the implant I found the only non-stop wouldn't get me to Charlotte until late afternoon and it would be an hour's drive to Darlynn from there. If I flew tomorrow and stayed overnight, I could meet with them the next day.

"I can be there Monday," I said to Marci. "What time of the day would be good for you?"

Marci was overjoyed that I could arrive so soon and was sure her Grandma would be too. She said that late morning would be good. We set the time at 10:00 a.m.

16.

"Why are you not having me take you there?" GERI asked. "I could have had you there in twenty minutes."

"I appreciate the offer, GERI. I don't know what I'm getting into. I don't want to have to explain to someone how I got to South Carolina so fast. I need to have this trip well documented."

"Good thinking," GERI said.

I asked him to investigate the lives of Marci Aherns and Myrtle Blackwell. Visiting them seemed safe enough, but everyone is a member of a network of other people. The others in the network of these two women might present a greater risk. It didn't take GERI long to investigate their network. Only one name stood out that might be a problem—Alan Roberts.

"He is Marci's ex-husband," GERI said. "It was an unhappy and short marriage according to the divorce papers. He was physically abusive among other things. He has a criminal record. Marci testified that she knew nothing about that when they got married and wanted the divorce as soon as she learned of it. Yesterday, a gas station was robbed in Liberty Hill, a town just across the county line from where Marci lives. The clerk was shot. Roberts is a person of interest. He is still at-large. The County Sheriff has a watch on Marci's house in case he goes there."

"You're right, GERI, that is important. We have already committed to the visit, so we will go. Why do I suddenly feel like I need to help those women? I hadn't met Marci before today and I just spoke with her for a few minutes."

"Is that a rhetorical question?" GERI asked.

"I guess it is. Well, Partner, I don't have a weapon besides my prodigious hand-to-hand combat skills. What do you have in case we need to defend ourselves or those damsels in distress?

"Did you use 'prodigious' flippantly, or do you have those skills? I would like our inventory of options to be accurate. I am not familiar with all the nuances of your conversation style."

"Both. I was making fun of myself, and I am skilled. How about you? What do you have?"

"I am an exploration unit. I am able to defend myself against all sorts of attacks. Also I have equipment to help me in my work—for example, a high-precision laser, sonic equipment to fracture stone, as well as other items that are useful."

"I don't know that we will encounter Roberts during our visit, but if we do, what do have to defend *me*. In science fiction books characters always seem to have a weapon that can be *set on stun*. Do you have anything like that?"

GERI laughed. He was getting better at it.

"Yes, I have something like that. The recipient of my weapon will fall to the ground unconscious when it is 'set on stun.' I do not think there is any lasting damage, but I imagine that the side effects are unpleasant. Also, I can project an impenetrable energy field, which I have used to avoid damage from an avalanche of stones. There are other aspects of my functionality we can explore at another time. The capabilities I have already listed should be sufficient to protect you, my friend."

"Thanks, GERI. Are there any other people associated with the family that we need to worry about?"

“No others stand out. It is possible that these women may encounter other problems.”

“What do you mean?”

“I am speculating that the money that you have found may belong to them, and that you will give it to them. If so, others may come forward, and attempt to take it from them.”

“Got it,” I said. “Let’s see what develops before we laser anyone.”

“Got it,” GERI said, and laughed again.

It was great having a cyber-based intelligence as a friend, especially one with a sense of humor. There were other benefits.

“GERI, when you researched my background before you tapped on my window that night, did you identify everywhere I was visible on the ‘grid’ as people call it?”

“Yes. Are you worried about something?”

“Not worried, but we are about to visit people about whom we know little. I don’t know what we might be getting into. I was wondering whether you found my fingerprints on record anywhere.”

“Yes. When you were in the Air Force, they took your fingerprints as part of approving your Top-Secret clearance. I found the record of your fingerprints in eight places.”

I pondered that for a moment. I had no reason to be worried about being identified based on what I usually do in my life. I was about to do something *unusual* and I didn’t know where it would lead. If I left no fingerprints on this upcoming trip and if fingerprint records were deleted, I would be doubly sure that my prints wouldn’t link me to whatever I got into. It would be like wearing a belt *and* suspenders.

“GERI, please delete the records of my fingerprints.”

“Done.”

“That was quick.”

"I relocated the records while you were thinking."

"Thanks."

"Are we planning to rob a bank?" he asked.

This time I laughed.

"No. I won't involve us in anything illegal, but I don't want to leave a trail back to us in case something happens. Fingerprints would be part of that trail."

"You'll leave prints while on your trip."

"I plan to wear gloves."

I owned a pair of close-fitting, black leather gloves. I also had a box of clear vinyl gloves I could use. They would both look odd. The clear ones would be less noticeable. If asked I could either say that I had a skin condition or that I was concerned about germs. I decided to go with the vinyl ones, but I'd bring the leather ones along.

On my drive back to town everything that had occurred today and over the last week rolled through my mind as an unorganized jumble. I was so distracted that I drove completely through Tipton—it doesn't take all that long—before I realized that I missed my turn to the Boarding House. I told my mind to get a grip and turned the SUV around.

I parked on the street in front of my temporary home with a sigh. It was noon. I went in wondering if Eleanor was fixing lunch. I shouldn't count on it. Lunch was not part of the room rent. I could always go to Mel's. I must have made enough noise for her to hear me enter. Of course, as she said before any noise not belonging to the Boarding House caught her attention.

"That you, Boarder Number 1?"

"Yes, Ma'am," I said, heading toward the sound of her voice coming from the kitchen.

"I hope you're not expecting lunch just because you show up at lunch time."

"No, Ma'am. I was just coming in to refresh myself from a rough morning at the farm. After that I was planning to go down the street to Mel's, to have lunch, and catch up on the *doings* in town."

Eleanor laughed.

"Well, I hate to take away one of Mel's few customers and rob you of the opportunity to 'catch up' on doings, but I have fixed lunch for both of us."

"A change in Boarding House rules?" I asked hopefully.

"We'll see. Now go do your refreshing. It's almost ready."

I came back a few minutes later and sat down to a savory smelling soup and an accompanying sandwich.

"When do you do your writing?" I asked.

I thought lunchtime conversation should at least start on the light side.

"There are usually a number of chores after breakfast, especially if there are demanding boarders around."

She gave me a look. Then she smiled and continued.

"It's quiet after that until it's time to fix the evening meal. That quiet time is best for me and my writing. On the days that Betty Saunders is here, I have even more time for it."

"It sounds like you really enjoy it."

"I do, Tom. It can be frustrating at times, but it's always a joy. I get very engaged with my characters. I laugh with them. I get scared when they do. Sometimes I cry with them."

As she said that, I saw a tear form in her eye. It was probably too personal a question, but I asked it anyway.

"Were you writing about something sad this morning?"

"Yes," she said. She lifted her linen napkin to her eye, took care of the tear, and then changed the subject.

"Tell me about your 'rough morning at the farm.'"

I told her about the joy of flying over the forest, and how I felt about what I saw.

"That's terrific, Tom, but it does not sound like that lasted very long, and it doesn't sound like a rough time. Did something else happen?"

"Yes. It was a full morning. Some of it you already know about. How are you doing with the news about the shooting?"

"Norm didn't stop by," she said. "It would have been nice to see him, but I was glad to avoid having to talk about it. I'm glad it's over. I'm trying to forget about it. What else happened out on your farm?"

I told her about the chamber and its contents. She laughed as I told her about the scramble to get it all concealed before Norm arrived.

"More money? Maybe I should raise the rent. What are you going to do?"

"I'm not sure. I don't think Agent Thomas would be pleased if I assumed that because the first batch of cash was of no interest to the FBI that they would have no interest in this new batch. So I might be contacting her and bringing her the money to have it examined, but that will have to wait."

"Why?"

I told her about Marci's call and the trip I would be taking tomorrow. I was pleased that I didn't have to elaborate on the potential danger of meeting up with Roberts. I thought she might worry. Heck, I was worried. I'd tell her about the trip after I have safely returned, hoping I would get the opportunity.

17.

I flew out Sunday morning and stayed overnight in Charlotte. I rented a car the next morning and left early enough to arrive in Darlynn in plenty of time. I had kept my vinyl gloves on while traveling on Sunday and had them on while was driving. I needed to stay in practice. GERI had arrived in Charlotte when I did and was following me to Darlynn.

"GERI, almost everywhere on this planet," I said, as I was driving, "there is the possibility that there will be a visual record of our activity captured via satellites."

"I have you covered, Tom," he said. "I have access to all satellites. I focus on those in orbit over any place we are. There will be no record of our presence stored in the satellites. In addition, I search for on-planet security cameras. I capture any in the area and shut them down while we are in their view."

That was reassuring.

"Let's review the plan," I said.

"I will hover over you wherever you are at all times," GERI said. "I will only act if you request something or if you need me to do something but are unable to make the request. Tom, does this activity that we are undertaking qualify for the moniker *cloak-and-dagger?* We have deleted your fingerprints. You are wearing gloves. I am blocking satellites and security cameras. I hope we get to do more of this. It is fun!"

"I think it does, but I don't share your enthusiasm for it. I'm the agent on the ground and potentially the one in the line-of-fire."

"Do not worry, Tom. I have got your six," GERI said, and laughed.

I was beginning to think that my cyber-friend had been compromised by reading too much human literature. "I've got your six?" In thrillers they used to say, "I've got your back." I guessed if I were looking forward, I would be looking at the twelve on the clock and "six" would be my back.

I arrived in Darlynn at 9:30 a.m. I called Marci and asked her if arriving a few minutes early would be alright. She said it was. I slowed down as I drove down the road where their home was located. It was an older neighborhood, with large sycamore trees lining both sides of the street. Their roots had pushed up parts of the sidewalks.

Marci's Grandma's home was in the middle of the block. It was one of the nicer homes and had been well taken care of. It was a vintage home that was probably built in the nineteen-forties. It had two stories, with gables and a covered porch across the front. The home had been painted recently. It was bright yellow with white trim, which highlighted the gingerbread fretwork under the front eaves covering the porch. It was up hill from the street, and there was a large front lawn that sloped down to the sidewalk. I walked up the broad set of stairs that led up to the porch. The front door had a tall oval of artistically etched glass set in a wooden frame that was painted white to match the trim. I rang the doorbell and waited for sound of activity within.

"Mr. Williams?" the young woman who answered the door inquired.

"Yes. Are you Marci?"

"Yes," she said, smiling. "Please come in. Grandma is in the sitting room. She is eager to talk with you."

According to our research Marci was thirty years old. She had lustrous, light-brown hair which hung in waves to her shoulders, and surrounded her bright, round face with its pink cheeks. She was about five-foot seven. She was wearing a yellow-print dress, which fitted her very well.

As Marci led me to her Grandma, I noticed that the furnishings matched the age of the house. The upholstery was in good shape, showing only minor signs of wear. There were lace doilies placed under everything on all of the wood surfaces.

Mrs. Blackwell was a slender woman who appeared to be in her late sixties or early seventies. Her thick hair was set in curls around her face. She had chosen to keep it colored brown. Whoever did the coloring did a fantastic job. The hair looked bright and alive. I didn't think she would like it if I said so, but she looked really good for her age. What captured my attention most were her beautiful smile and the energy in her lovely, hazel eyes.

"Mr. Williams, I am glad to make your acquaintance," Mrs. Blackwell said, with a surprisingly strong, if quiet voice. "Please sit down."

They had arranged three chairs around a small table. The chair Mrs. Blackwell was sitting in looked like it might be her regular one. Marci and I sat in the other two.

"Thank you, Mrs. Blackwell. I'm also glad to meet you."

"Call me Myrtle, please. You are going to know more about me and mine before we are done. Let's go to first names right away. What do you say?"

"Good idea. Please call me Tom."

"Tom, Marci has fixed some iced tea, would you like some?"

I nodded and Marci poured the tea into the glasses on the table. I lifted my glass and took a sip. The two women did the same. They noticed my vinyl gloves, but they didn't ask about them.

"Where shall we begin?" I asked.

"Why don't you tell us what you found," Myrtle said. "If it is what I think it is, I'll tell you the story behind it."

I was about to begin when I got an alert from GERI.

"Tom, the police have just determined that Roberts is headed this way. I have spotted his car. He will be there in a few minutes. I do not think the Sheriff's men can get there any sooner than ten minutes."

I touched the side of my head as if I were getting a message.

"Tom, what is it?" Marci asked.

"I can't explain how I know these things, but here it is. Your ex-husband, Alan Roberts, robbed a gas station in Liberty Hill two days ago. The clerk was shot. The Sheriff didn't know where Roberts was, so he had a watch put on the approaches to your home in case he came here. Roberts is on his way. He will be here in just a few minutes. The Sheriff won't get here soon enough."

"Liberty Hill is over in Kershaw County," Myrtle said.

"Yes," I said. "I will go out and meet him."

Marci looked terrified. I didn't blame her. Myrtle didn't look afraid. She'd probably had faced many things in her life.

"But why are you getting involved?" Marci stammered out. "He may hurt you."

"We can't let him in here. I believe I can keep him from hurting anyone."

I hoped that was true. I heard a car pull up outside. I got up from my chair and raced out the front door. He was getting out of the car and rushing toward the front of the house. He was wearing a white tee shirt and blue jeans and looked haggard.

"Mr. Roberts! I need to talk with you," I said, holding up my hand.

He was bigger than I expected—taller than me and weighed more.

"Out of my way!" he shouted.

"Stop, Roberts! I'm not going to let you endanger those two women in the house. So you have two options. You can keep running, or you can give yourself up when the Sheriff gets here."

"You called the Sheriff!" He shouted and looked like he was going to pull a weapon out of his waistband in the back of his pants.

"No. They have had a watch on this place. They spotted you coming this way. You have just a few minutes to make up your mind."

"Out of my way! If I get into that house I can hide."

"I'm not going to let you in, and your car will show them that you are still here anyway. Listen, I know something you don't know. The clerk did not die. You'll be facing armed robbery, but not murder. The Sheriff's men will still assume that you are armed. If you run, they are authorized to use lethal force. That means they may kill you."

"They'll shoot me either way."

"Not if you put down your weapon and let them take you without resisting. I'll make sure of that. I'm filming what we are doing out here."

"What? How are you doing that? Who are you anyway? Why are you here?"

"Good, he's talking," I thought and sent to GERI. "Keep watching, but we may have this going in the right direction."

"I'm here visiting Mrs. Blackwell on another matter. Before I came, I checked out the family which used to include you. Once I found out your situation, I've been listening in on the Sheriff's communications. Hear that siren? You have less than two minutes to make up your mind. If you still have that weapon in the back of your pants when they get here, things might get nasty fast. What are you going to do?"

He drew out his weapon. I knew GERI was watching as intently as I was, but I was nervous just the same. He looked at the gun, then at me. The siren was getting closer.

"Shit! Shit! I don't know!"

"Throw it down right now. It's your only real chance to live out the day, Alan."

To my surprise he threw it about eight feet to his right.

"You will still look dangerous to them standing there. I suggest that you lay down on your stomach with your hands stretched out to the side. That's the position they will want you in when they cuff you.

He did it! Ten seconds later, a Sheriff's car raced down the middle of the street, siren blaring and lights flashing, and screeched to a tire-smoking stop in front of the house.

18.

Two Sheriff's Deputies jumped out of the patrol car, drew their weapons, and ducked down behind their car door. Two more Sheriff's cars raced into the street and stopped out front. I didn't want to appear threatening, so I sat down on the front step.

"Deputies," I shouted and waved. "Over here. My name is Tom Williams. I wanted you to know right away that Mr. Roberts has chosen to turn himself in. He's on the lawn in front of you. He tossed his gun on the lawn away to his right."

One of the first Deputies to arrive stood up where he was near his patrol car and looked around. Cautiously the other deputy did the same. Two deputies came out of each of the two new patrol cars. All six were carefully converging on the front lawn. Once the first deputy saw that I was telling the truth, he raced up to Roberts, cuffed him and read him his rights. His partner retrieved Roberts' gun. At first, they had Roberts in a sitting position. Shortly after that, two other deputies took Roberts to their car and locked him in the back seat.

The first deputy on the scene came over to me and introduced himself as Deputy Dickerson.

"What's you name again, sir?"

"Williams," I said. "Tom Williams."

"What is your involvement with this situation?"

"I was visiting Ms. Aherns and Mrs. Blackwell when Roberts pulled up. I knew who he was and that he was on the run. I came out here, to make sure he didn't get into the house."

"Did you know he was armed?" the Deputy asked.

I nodded.

"He didn't try to force his way into the house?" the Deputy asked.

"He was scared," I said. "He didn't have a plan. He was afraid you were going to shoot him. Once I got him talking, he seemed to listen. I told him that his best chance to live was to end this by turning himself in. He was probably hungry and looked like he hadn't slept. What little energy he had left went out of him. He seemed to realize what I said was true. He threw his gun aside, laid down on the lawn and spread his arms out like you saw."

"Are you a friend of the family?"

"No, Sir, this is the first time I've met with them."

"And yet, you…"

"Deputy, it had to be done. Roberts had a gun and there were two defenseless women inside. You would have done the same thing."

He nodded, seeing the truth of the matter. He asked about my gloves. I told him I wore them when traveling to avoid germs. He obviously thought it odd but didn't ask me anymore questions.

"Shall we go in?" he gestured toward the front door. "By the way I've met Mrs. Blackwell before. I can't picture her as a 'defenseless woman,' and I don't imagine she'd like being characterized that way."

I smiled and said, "I've only spoken with her for a brief time, but I agree with you."

The Deputy and I went in the house. Both women had risen and had been looking out the window since Roberts first pulled up. The Deputy took our statements and said that his department would send someone to tow Roberts' car to their impound lot.

After he had left and all the patrol cars had departed, the three of us stood looking at each other. Actually Marci and Myrtle were looking at me.

"You need to change your pants, Tom?" Myrtle asked with a mischievous smile.

"Grandma!" Marci shouted, scandalized at her Grandma's colorful remark.

"No, but it was a close thing, Myrtle," I said and laughed.

They joined in. We all needed to relax after what had just happened.

"Shall we get back to our iced tea," I suggested.

After sitting down it was clear that Marci had not recovered from the shock of recent events. Myrtle saw that. She reached over and put her hand on Marci's.

"Why don't you take a moment, child," she said. "Go refresh yourself. Maybe put a warm washcloth on the back of your neck and on your face."

Marci nodded thankful for the break. After she had gone Myrtle turned to me and asked, "What were you thinking, running out there like that, Tom?"

"You know we couldn't let him in the house, Myrtle. I learned that he could be dangerous when I researched all of you. He had to be stopped out there."

She looked me in the eyes for a moment, and then nodded and sipped her tea.

"So are you going to tell me how you know about us, and how you knew as soon as the Sheriff did that Alan was heading this way?"

"I don't want to lie to you, Myrtle. So instead I will say I can't tell you. I hope you can accept that."

"Some kind of hi-tech secret?"

"Yes, something along those lines."

"I can live with that," she said. "I think we should wait for Marci before starting with the details. Perrin International Banking has been on my mind for a long time, but she has only recently been involved. She set up the technology that sent us a message that you had shown an interest in Perrin."

I decided to wait to mention that the FBI couldn't find or trace Marci's technology. Marci should hear how successful her work had been.

Marci came back in and sat down. Myrtle looked at her. Satisfied that her granddaughter was alright she turned to me.

"Let's begin again. What did you find, Tom?"

I told them about the first batch of money but didn't mention the gold. I needed to think about that.

"Since the FBI cleared the cash from any illegal activity," I said, "I put it in a separate bank account until I found out more about it. By the way Marci, the FBI found my inquiry into Perrin, but not yours. They thought that whatever it was might have triggered a message, but that was just a guess. Myrtle told me that was your work. Well done!"

"Is that all you found?" Myrtle asked, with an intense look on her face.

I told them about the bank information.

"I didn't want to touch it, but with your skills, Marci, you might be able to check to see if the balance is real and if you can draw it out somehow."

She nodded and smiled, obviously pleased that her part played an important role already and there might be more for her to do.

"Then out in the barn…" I went on to tell them about the chamber and cash, again leaving out the precious metals. I said that I believed that I would also have to ask the FBI to check on the serial numbers of the cash.

Myrtle sighed and said, "They won't find anything on that money either."

We both looked at Myrtle expectantly.

"Can I know about it now, Grandma?" Marci asked.

"Yes, dear," Myrtle said, with a sympathetic smile for her granddaughter. "It can all be told now. I think the mystery has finally come full circle.

"My husband, Bobby, was a wonderful man, but he wasn't a good businessman, and he was gullible. He was swindled in a big way over thirty years ago now. I was there, but he had hidden what he was doing from me. I think he wanted to show me that he could carry off a big deal on his own. That's not an excuse, but an explanation why I hadn't stopped the swindle before it ruined us.

"We owned and operated Delta National bank in Mississippi. We were located in a small town, but there were a number of rich cotton farmers in the area and nearly all of them banked with us. We kept an unusually large amount of cash on hand because many of the farmers liked to do some of their business on a cash-only basis. We had to be ready to provide hundreds of thousands of dollars in cash on a moment's notice. So we usually had several million dollars in our vault. It was a risk to have that much on hand, but that was part of our business.

"The man who swindled us used a different name, but he sounds very much like the man, Simpson, you told us about. It must be the same man, because he still had what was left of the cash in the original wrappers.

Simpson came to my husband and told him how he could double his money almost overnight by investing in commodities, such as cotton futures and other similar investments. Bobby was enthralled. He knew I would never go along with such a scheme, so he had to come up with the money some other way.

"Since the man said the profit would be made very quickly, Bobby thought he could use the money out of our vault. Of course it wasn't our money, but our customers' deposits. Bobby knew that but thought that he would get it back before anyone noticed it was missing.

"Bobby wanted to make a bundle, so he took over a million dollars from the vault and gave it to Simpson. That was the last Bobby ever saw of the man. After he handed the money over to Simpson, Bobby tried to contact him, but he never received any response. Simpson had lived in town when working with Bobby. He left without a trace."

"I looked into Delta National," I said. "It closed its doors thirty years ago, but there was no mention of it being robbed."

"It wasn't robbed. No one ever knew what happened. My family came from this part of South Carolina, Tom. We were a family of successful textile merchants. When my parents died, I was the sole heir, and I had to run the textile business here. I had to split my time between here and Mississippi. That was another reason that I didn't catch on to what was happening.

"When I found out what Bobby had done, I quickly took money from my textile business and put it into the Delta National vaults. We alerted our bank customers that we were going to close the bank. We made good on all of our obligations and closed the doors.

"Taking that money from our textile operation ultimately caused me to have to close down the business. I wasn't penniless, but I had lost a lot of money, and people who had worked for my family for years lost their jobs.

"Bobby had grown up in that part of Mississippi. With my help, he had started Delta National and we lived there. Many of our farmer customers knew Bobby and his family. When Bobby saw what his foolish action had done to me, the bank he had started, and my family's textile business, he couldn't live with it. He took his own life."

"That must have been terrible for you, Grandma," Marci said, with tears in her eyes.

"It was, Marci. I got through it, but I never got over it."

Marci teared up again. I waited for the moment to pass before asking my question.

"How does the Perrin bank enter into it?"

"Ah, Perrin International Bank," Myrtle said. "As part of the swindle Simpson showed Bobby that his money had been deposited into an account at that bank. I don't think there is such a bank. Marci can check it out, but I don't think there is anything to it."

19.

I was inclined to agree with Myrtle. Still it should be checked out. I went out to my car to get the bank information. It was still sunny out. Birds were chirping in the sycamores. Other than Robert's car at the curb, there was no evidence of the earlier drama. Neighbors were standing on the sidewalk talking over what they had seen. One of them, a man who looked like he was in his seventies came over to me as I approached my car.

"You're the guy who talked that fella into giving himself up to the Sheriff?"

"Yes, Sir."

"Weren't you scared?"

"Yes, Sir."

"Myrtle and her granddaughter, are they okay?"

"Yes, Sir, though I don't think this is a good time to talk with them."

"Yeah, I guess you're right about that. If you say they're okay now, I'll check on them later, maybe tomorrow."

"They've had a shock," I said. "Tomorrow might be best."

He nodded his head and went back to the others. I hadn't told him anything, but they were eager to hear whatever he had learned from me. I went to the car and retrieved the envelope with the bank information from the front seat.

When I came in Myrtle was standing at the door.

"That was Jimmy Ray Larson, who came up to you. I've known him for years. He lives next door. It's natural he'd want to know I was okay."

"He *was* concerned. I told him that talking to you tomorrow would be best. He'll probably be over as soon as I leave."

"I imagine you're right, Tom. Jimmy Ray thinks a 'woman my age' needs looking after. He's been trying to do that since his wife died seven years ago. He's a sweet old man, but he can be a pest. His visits have become less frequent since Marci moved in two years ago. His excuse that I needed looking after went away since Marci was here doing that very thing."

She looked at the envelope. "Is that the bank information?"

"Yes."

"You can give it to Marci. We need to talk about the cash now, Tom."

We went over to where Marci was still sitting. I handed her the envelope.

"There is one thing that puzzles me about the bank, Myrtle. The FBI has a file with that name on it. If the matter at Delta National was never reported, why is the FBI looking for anything to do with Perrin?"

Myrtle looked at me for a moment as if deciding whether to tell me something.

"Oh, well, since he's dead now it won't do him any harm."

"Who, Grandma?"

"A family friend, Marci, a dear friend, Mr. Samuel Baker. Sam grew up around here. He was younger than me, but all of us kids always played together. Sam joined the FBI after college, and I lost track of him.

"When Bobby killed himself, Sam heard about it. He was working out of the FBI office in Memphis. He came to me in Mississippi and asked if there was anything he could do for me.

I told him that I couldn't tell him anything about it, but it would be a great favor to me if he would have the FBI look for anything with Perrin's name on it. He was a senior agent, so he was able to put the name on their watch list without anyone asking questions. It was a surprise to me, Tom, when you said that they were still looking into it."

"The agent I spoke with told me that the FBI never drops anything until it's over. She didn't know anything about the file."

"Are you going to tell her now that you know?" Myrtle asked.

"I don't want to, but their involvement complicates things."

"Ah yes, the cash," Myrtle said. "What are your plans for the money, Tom?"

"Now that I know the story, Myrtle, I want you to have it. Let's talk about how we can get it to you. Maybe we'll see a way to avoid disclosing the details to the FBI."

"Why would they need to be involved?" Marci asked.

"The cash, Marci," Myrtle said. "The FBI needs to confirm that it wasn't part of something illegal, like a bank robbery or a drug deal. Isn't that right, Tom?"

"Yes, and if we hide this new batch of cash, it will show up when you try to deposit it. Then the FBI will be interested in why we were hiding it from them."

Marci looked like she was going to ask another question. Myrtle told her about the requirement to report large cash deposits. Then Myrtle paused, apparently thinking about what she had just said. I probably didn't want to know what she was thinking. She had dealt with large cash transactions in her banking days. Her customers had been "farmers" who dealt in "cash-only" transactions. Hmmm. She may have skirted around the regulations back then. How could I deal with a seventy-something ex-banker who had done money laundering on the side?

Myrtle got a look in her eye and a smile on her face that made me think my suspicions were on target. She didn't show me her cards.

"You say you already have banked the first batch you found, Tom?"

"Yes, Ma'am."

"Good. I'll give you an account to which you can wire that money."

"Yes, Ma'am"

She was thinking, and either didn't notice or chose to ignore my repetitive responses. I was hoping it was the former.

"Now about the cash," she continued, as if thinking out loud, "when can you get that to me."

Maybe I wouldn't be an accomplice if I just handed her the money. Though I would still be nervous having neglected to tell Agent Thomas about finding the second stash.

"I can deliver it tomorrow if you will tell me where I can put that much cash without anyone noticing."

"That won't be a problem," she said. She was in a groove now.

"Marci get our things. We're going to visit the Mill."

Marci jumped up. So did I. I figured Myrtle was not done with me yet. She was also taking me to the 'Mill.'

"Interesting," GERI said over my implant. He was still hovering invisible above the house.

"Yes," I thought back to him.

I didn't have time for more. Marci was helping Myrtle with her coat, and they were heading toward the back of the house.

"We have Grandma's car in the garage," Marci said. "Please follow us when we come out to the street."

I was happy to see that Marci was driving the vintage silver Bentley when they pulled out onto the street. The sight of such a car had me recalibrating Myrtle's comment that she "wasn't penniless" after the events of thirty years ago.

The old textile mill was only a fifteen-minute drive from Myrtle's home. There was a tall, wrought-iron fence surrounding the five-acre property. The gate in the fence opened to let us through at the approach of the Bentley.

The textile mill was everything I envisioned when GERI had described it to me. It was a two-story, dark-red brick building. It was over one hundred feet long and fifty feet wide. There were windows along both sides just under the eaves. It also had a number of windows along the walls seven feet off the ground, which would let in daylight and fresh air for the workers. The building had been well-maintained and looked good for a building that had been closed for thirty years. There were other smaller buildings inside the fence. The buildings and the fence had also been well taken care of.

The place looked like it could start up at any minute. It wasn't hard to imagine workers walking about and hearing the machines spinning inside. I parked my car next to theirs. When I stepped out onto the pavement all I heard was the birds chirping and the wind rustling the leaves of the trees that had been planted outside the fence all around the property.

Marci helped her grandma out of the car, though she didn't appear to need much help. Whatever age Myrtle was, she was in control of today's events.

We had parked at the end of the building where the office was. Marci unlocked the door, and we all went in. Marci walked around switching on lights and checking equipment. The office was filled with server racks. There was a well-equipped workstation on an expensive looking desk. I turned to Marci.

"Is this your office?"

"Yes. I do odd jobs for Grandma and a few other clients."

It was becoming clear that I was not visiting some quiet-living, young woman who was taking care of her aging grandmother. I hoped they didn't tell me about the "odd jobs" or who the other clients were. The *aging* grandmother was already heading out of Marci's office into what was obviously Myrtle's office. We followed her in there.

Myrtle had stopped at one end of the large office facing an inside wall. She touched something and part of the wood paneling slid to the side revealing a solid steel door. It had a modern keypad lock on it. Myrtle punched in a sixteen-digit code. The inch-thick steel door popped open. Myrtle swung it out effortlessly on the door's solid, internal, frictionless hinges.

I didn't want to be nosy, so I stood where I was. Myrtle motioned for Marci and me to follow her. When I came to the entrance, what I saw would not be called a vault in the banking sense. It was more of a *strong room.* Its concrete walls were lined with steel plate on the inside. I noticed on the way in that the inside surface of the wall panel that slid aside, and the concrete enclosure were covered with a metal mesh screen which itself was covered with a thin, plastic-looking film. I wondered why they would need an additional intrusion-proof cover—more than your ordinary strong room then.

The inside was twenty feet long and ten feet wide. Although the room itself was constructed of concrete-covered steel, the inside had wood paneling and shelves. The center isle was three feet wide. Lying on the shelves were flat wood boxes made of artfully crafted dark wood, which might contain jewelry or precious gems. There were also gold and silver ingots—a sight I was getting accustomed to. In addition, there were small assemblies of various shapes and sizes, enclosed in metal with buttons, switches and lights which were not lit. I guessed that these were sensitive electronic devices of some kind that might be the reason for the intrusion-proofing. There was an open space at the end of the room. Myrtle pointed to it.

"That is where we will put the cash when you deliver it," she said.

20.

I looked at the space and then to Myrtle. I was trying to absorb all that I had seen in the past few minutes. My absorption rate, like my metabolism rate, was getting slower. I gave up.

"Looks like it will fit there," I said. "Can you show me where I can enter the Mill to bring it in?"

We went back into Marci's office then through a door into a large space where all the textile machines were spread across the floor on the right. On the left there was an empty space going from where we stood to the end of the building forty feet away. There was a large, metal, roll-up door on the end of the building. We walked to where the door controls were. Myrtle pushed a large red button in a metal electrical switch box. The door rolled up completely to the ceiling thirty feet above.

"We'll meet you here, and open this door for you," Myrtle said. "You can drive your vehicle in here and unload."

I was still trying to figure out how I was going to do the delivery. It would be awkward to take it from GERI, put it in the rental car, and then unload it here. The main awkwardness was finding a place where I wouldn't be seen unloading GERI. I asked GERI if he had any ideas.

"I think you're going to have to figure that one out yourself," he said.

"Thanks for the help."

"You're the agent on the ground," GERI said, and laughed.

I was thinking that I might grow tired of that laugh. I decided to try the only thing I thought might work.

"I will call you when I arrive, Myrtle. I will need you to go into your office after you open this door. I'll let you know when I've unloaded and it's alright to come out."

"Why is that?" Myrtle asked.

She was smiling, so I don't think I raised any suspicions. I think she was having fun putting me on the spot.

"We've only known each other for a few hours," I began, "but in that time I've come to like you and Marci. Perhaps you feel the same toward me. Still, from what I've seen of your operation here, I believe we both have things we wish to keep secret. How I am going to deliver the cash is one of the things I need to keep secret."

Marci looked to her grandmother, with a questioning and worried look on her face. Myrtle held onto the silence for effect. Then she laughed, loud and long.

"Okay, Tom. You just let us know when you arrive. We'll go hide our eyes in the office. I am dearly curious, but you're right. We both have our secrets."

"I think she is lying about not viewing us when we unload the cash," GERI said.

"I agree. We'll have to deal with that when we get here," I responded.

I liked Myrtle more as time went on, but that didn't mean I trusted her. We set a time for my arrival the next day. I wouldn't be using a rental car, so I could come directly to Darlynn. I don't know what I'd do if they asked me to stay for dinner.

We left the Mill property at the same time. I drove back to Charlotte and arrived in time to catch my return flight to Seattle and drove back to Tipton. I felt apprehensive about the trip to

South Carolina tomorrow, but at least it would be faster. I'd be flying in GERI.

Arriving in Tipton made me remember that I would have to deal with rumors in a small town. I parked in front of the Boarding House. I heard several excited voices discussing something as I came up the step. Looking through the window in the door, I saw Eleanor was standing in the foyer with three women around her. I heard her voice over the others.

"You'll just have to ask him when he gets here," she said.

It looked like Eleanor was glad to see me when I came in the door. I could imagine why. I was the "him" that her visitors were going to have to "ask." I was willing to bet that this had to do with the rumor that Norm was talking about.

They all turned to me when I came in. I recognized two of the visitors, and thought I also knew the name of the third. I thought I better start talking to try to stay ahead of the storm.

"Let me see," I said looking at the women as if I was trying to guess who they were. All three had been in my class in high school.

I pointed to the smaller one with black hair and a slender figure. I knew her as Nina Whitehorse, but I thought I should stay with first names. "You're Nina, aren't you?"

She nodded. I went to the next two. "And you are Louisa and you're Frankie?"

Louisa and Frankie could have been sisters, they looked so similar. They were both five-foot eight, with brown wavy hair. Louisa wore hers long and Frankie's was cut short.

"I go by Francis now, Tom."

"You three haven't changed at all since I saw you last."

"You haven't changed either, Tom," Louisa said, "still trying to charm your way out of something."

I went over and hugged all of them. Nina and Francis hugged me back lightly. Louisa gave me a big welcoming hug. I was a little flustered by so much female attention, but I soldiered on.

“From what Eleanor was saying when I came in, it sounds like you might be here to see me.”

“That’s right, Tom,” Nina said. “Don’t try to act like you can’t imagine why we want to talk with you.”

“Why don’t you tell me, anyway.”

Louisa said, “It’s all around town that you found some money out at the Simpson place. We wanted to talk with you about that. Others thought it would be better to have someone who you knew when it came to discussing it. So we volunteered since we all knew you from school.”

I looked to Eleanor. She smiled and gave me a you’re-on-your-own look and winked.

We all went into the dining room and sat down.

“Let’s start at the beginning,” I said. “I did find some money. What do you want to talk with me about?”

“We were wondering if you could tell us about it, and maybe what you were going to do with it,” Louisa said.

I told them what I had found, except for the gold bars. I said I had brought it to the FBI and why. I ended by saying that I put it in the bank. I didn’t elaborate. I didn’t want the money to begin with, and now I knew it belonged to someone else. There was silence when I finished with the discussion. I let that go on for a while and then began again.

“I imagine that you know that I had asked Rachel if she wanted it.”

“Yes, and we don’t blame her for not wanting anything to do with it,” Francis said.

"Now you know about the money I found. I'll also say that I did look around and couldn't find any more money in the house in case anyone in town is wondering about that," I stated with a calm voice. I tried to avoid sounding like I thought it wasn't any of their business, though I did think that. Maybe I should have acted angry because they went further.

"What do you plan to do with it?" Nina asked.

"What do you mean? I told you what I did with it. I put it in the bank."

"We were wondering…," Louisa began, "I mean those in the town were wondering…."

"Wondering what, Louisa? Please speak plainly."

"Well it occurred to some that it was found money, you know extra money that you hadn't counted on getting in the deal when you bought the place. We were wondering if you could use it to help out people in need here in town."

I had been thinking about something similar since I had arrived in Tipton a week ago. This might be an opportunity to carry it out, so I said, "I see. Since you're the delegation that was sent to present the town's case, I suggest that you put together a proposal and that we talk about it tomorrow evening. It doesn't have to be an elaborate presentation, but I would like to see your ideas on how this would work. I haven't said I'd do anything yet, but let's talk about it. Eleanor can we meet here after we're done with dinner tomorrow evening?"

The faces of the delegation showed relief and elation at the same time. Eleanor said we could. The delegation looked like they were floating on air as they went out the front door.

"I haven't eaten yet, Tom, but everything is ready," Eleanor said.

I reached out and gently squeezed her hand. I was so glad to be here with her, and now she said we were going to have dinner together. I looked at her. I'm sure she could see how grateful I was that she had said that.

"Thanks, Eleanor. I'll go wash up and I'll be right back."

She smiled and said, "There's red wine on the bureau."

"Thanks, and I know," I said, "dinner is something that goes with red wine."

She smiled and went into the kitchen.

"I was back downstairs before she had brought the food, so I poured wine in both of our glasses at the place settings. I lifted mine and took a sip as she was bringing in a large bowl of pasta with fresh tomato-based sauce and vegetables.

When we sat down to eat Eleanor said, "I hope you don't get tired of this pasta dish. It's easy to fix and you seem to like it."

"Well, I suggest that we change to a butter, garlic and white wine sauce in summer. Until then I hope you don't get tired of cooking this. I really do love it."

Eleanor asked about my South Carolina trip. I told her everything including my talking Roberts into giving himself up. When she exclaimed that I shouldn't have taken the risk I knew she understood why I had to do it. We were quiet for a while. I could almost guess what her next question was going to be. I was right.

"Wait a minute, Tom. If you're going to give the money to that woman in South Carolina, why are you letting my friends think that you might give it to them?"

I looked at her. She was beautiful, had a smile that could melt icebergs, was running a small business, was a successful writer, and she still had space in her heart to look out for her friends.

I must have taken too long to answer her question. She started tapping her finger on the table and asked, "Well, Mr. Williams?"

I had to tell her more, but I wanted to avoid telling her how wealthy I was. I could ease into that later.

"I am going to give Myrtle the cash from the house and the barn, but not the gold that I found. I didn't tell Myrtle about that because I didn't see that it was hers, exactly. What I'll do is turn the gold into cash, put it in the bank, and let your friends, I mean our friends use that."

"Will that be enough?"

"Yes, more than enough."

She was pleased our friends wouldn't be disappointed. She smiled and reached over and squeezed my hand. "This is a very nice thing you are doing, Tom." We clinked our wine glasses.

I didn't tell her the rest of my plan.

21.

"What do I tell people about where you are?" Eleanor asked at breakfast. "Your SUV will be at the farm, but you won't."

"It's going to be cold today, but rain isn't likely. You can say I'm in the forest if it comes up," I said. "I'll work on a better way of handling my absences."

"Okay," she said. "Will there be any danger this time?"

"Nope," I assured her.

I hoped I sounded confident because I wasn't. Working with Myrtle Blackwell might bring surprises, and some of those could be dangerous. It looked like her operation might have a bit of a shady side to it.

I drove to the farm and parked outside the barn. When I went in I looked around. The bales of hay were still over the trap door. Nothing seemed disturbed. Of course, GERI would have let me know if anyone had been there.

When GERI is invisible, there is no way for me to know where he is. The only sound he made was a barely detectable hum. This morning I didn't hear the hum above the noise my boots were making on the dusty barn floor. So I nearly jumped when he appeared directly in front of me.

"Nice. Are you going to be doing that a lot?"

GERI laughed.

"Do you know what a cowbell is?" I asked.

He laughed again. I knew I wasn't going to win against the brightest intelligence on the planet, so I gave up. I asked GERI to move out of the barn. I locked the door and asked if there was anyone around us. When GERI said we were alone, I climbed in, put my gloves on and we headed for South Carolina.

We arrived in Darlynn at 12:30 p.m., thirty minutes ahead of when we had agreed to meet. I was glad I had. We hovered over Myrtle's home waiting for her Bentley to come out and drive to the Mill. There was a black SUV parked at the curb. The front door of the house opened. Marci and Myrtle came out followed by two men in gray suits. It didn't look like a friendly gathering. The two men put Marci and Myrtle into the back seat of the SUV. They got into the front and drove away.

"Can your sensors detect any weapons on those men, GERI? They would likely be small metal items."

"The two men have weapons," GERI said. "Myrtle and Marci do not."

"That sounds unfriendly," I said.

"What is next?" GERI asked, with a little too much enthusiasm.

"GERI this looks like a real cloak-and-dagger situation. Our friends might be injured. I might be injured."

"I know, Tom, but it is exciting even so. Shall I set my weapon on stun?"

I chuckled.

"It would be a good idea to have that weapon of yours ready. How precise is the aiming of it anyway?"

"It can be applied broadly or in a narrow beam. The weapon attacks the nervous system. In tight situations where others are near, I would aim the beam at the target's brain. Its effective range is one-hundred fifty feet."

"Can it go through walls?"

"Yes, but it is not effective that way. The strength is unpredictable, the beam broadens and aiming is not accurate."

"Thanks, GERI. I think our next step is to follow them."

The SUV went to the Mill. When they arrived, Marci got out and entered a code into the gate control. It opened. Marci walked to the office. The SUV drove around to the end of the building. We followed right behind it. The metal roll-up door rose, and the SUV went in. I knew we were going to have to act fast if we were going to do anything before the door went down. I gave GERI some instructions.

When Myrtle and the men exited the SUV, GERI made a loud noise like a horn. The two men turned around and drew their weapons. GERI captured their images and then stunned them. They dropped to the ground.

Myrtle was startled. I called her on her phone.

"Myrtle, it's me, Tom."

"Did you kill these men?"

"It was me, but they are unconscious, not dead. I assumed that you were in danger."

"I was. Thank you."

Marci came out. When she saw the men on the floor, she ran over and hugged Myrtle. Myrtle comforted her for a moment before talking to me again.

"Where are you?" Myrtle asked.

"I can't tell you that. If you can bear with me a bit longer, I need to ask you and Marci to go into the office, and 'hide your eyes' as you said yesterday. I will unload the cash and take care of the men."

"Alright," she said. She was obviously relieved, but still on her feet. "You have some explaining to do, Tom."

"So do you, Myrtle. Now please go inside. I'll let you know when it's okay to come out."

Myrtle led Marci into the office.

"What is your plan?" GERI asked.

"I don't have a plan. Let's unload the cash while I develop one."

I got out of GERI and went to the back and started moving the cash to a spot near the door to Marci's office. By the time I was done, I thought I had a fairly good plan. GERI had given me the information that these two were wanted in Charlotte in connection with a murder there.

"How long will they be out?"

"Definitely two hours," GERI said. "Maybe longer."

"Okay, let's get these men into the back of their SUV."

I dropped the back seats flat and opened the hatch at the back. GERI was able to lift each man up and lay them on the large area in the back of the SUV. I closed the hatch. I spotted a roll of paper about three feet wide leaning against the wall. I tore off a ten-foot piece. I put the paper on the floor of the SUV and over the driver's seat. I got in and backed it out of the Mill. GERI asked me if I wanted to blank out coverage of the SUV as I drove it away. I told him I wanted the SUV visible.

I called Myrtle.

"You can come out and start moving the cash into your strong room. I have the men in their SUV and I'm going to drive it away. I'll be back in about an hour."

"Tom, I can't thank you enough. Please come back and tell me how things went. I promise to tell you what happened this morning."

I said I would and drove out of the gate. I headed north toward Charlotte. I'd driven thirty minutes when I spotted what I was looking for. It was a shopping mall with a multi-level parking lot. I drove into the underground level and hunted for a spot with few cars. GERI followed me in. I asked him to check the area for other people and to block the cameras. Once he assured me it was clear, I got out of the SUV taking the paper with me, left the keys on the front seat, and got into GERI who had landed right next to me. We left the lot and headed back toward the Mill.

"Will these men need medical attention, GERI?"

"They might, Tom. I have never used this weapon on a human. Actually, I have never used the weapon on anyone."

"What! You might have told me."

"I was confident it would work because..."

"…because you designed it."

"Yes."

We sent an anonymous message to the Charlotte police telling them of the location of the men, that they were armed and that they might need medical attention.

I called Myrtle and told her I'd meet her at the Mill. When we arrived, I had GERI drop me off outside the fence.

I walked through the open gate and into the office. Apparently they had been watching me.

"Why didn't you just fly into the parking lot in your invisible plane or whatever it is?" Myrtle asked, with a smirk on her face.

"What are you talking about, Myrtle?" I asked incredulously. "I think you've been watching too much TV."

"I'll show you what I'm talking about, Mr. Williams," she said smugly.

Myrtle turned to Marci and said, "Run the recording, Marci."

Marci used her keyboard to bring up the security recording. They were surprised that the screen was blank. Earlier while I was unloading the cash and we loaded the men into the SUV, GERI had been working on the security system in the Mill.

"But we saw you," Myrtle exclaimed.

"What did you see, Myrtle? Whatever you think you saw doesn't exist, and no one would believe you if you tried to tell them about it. In addition to that segment, we've deleted all of the security recordings starting two weeks ago, which includes the section that shows I was here yesterday."

When she started to protest, I raised my hand.

"There wasn't anything of importance on them. Hear me out. I didn't want a recording of my activity today, but there is more. Those men were criminals wanted by the Charlotte police. You can explain why they were with you to me, but you are also likely to have to explain it to the police. We've told the police where to find them. It probably won't end there.

"When the men awake, they will find themselves in custody. They will be questioned by the police. Their answers might lead back to you. Even if what they say doesn't lead directly to you, the authorities can find you. If they look at satellite coverage of the area, they will be able to trace the SUV to your house, and then to the Mill. The next segment will show the SUV leaving here and going to the underground parking lot where we left them. As far as the police will be able to tell, those men were driving the SUV the whole time.

"If the police come to you, they will ask you why they were here and why they left so soon after arriving. You'll need to have an answer and it will help if you don't have any security recordings that you have to explain. With two weeks of blank recordings, you can say that it must have failed, or that you knew it was broken, but just hadn't fixed it yet. You'll still have to explain why they were here."

Myrtle wasn't easily spooked, but this had thrown her.

"Who are you?" she asked, with a look of disbelief on her face.

"I'm just an ordinary guy, who was doing you a good deed by returning your money and helping you out of some trouble.

"When they look into things, the police will find I visited you yesterday. As far as they know I was not here today. When asked I will tell them about the first batch of money I found. I suggest that we keep the batch I delivered today out of the discussion. If you have to show it to someone sometime you can claim you've had it all the time since your banking days.

"Now we need to figure out what you are going to say about your visitors."

"I agree we should keep today's money out of the discussion," Myrtle said. "Those men had learned that I had money, probably from one of my clients. They were looking for a good opportunity to take some of it. They must have planted a listening device in my home somehow and had learned about your delivery today as a result. They were going to take that money and anything else that was available. They threatened to kill us if we didn't cooperate."

"If you keep today's delivery out of that, you can say they forced you to come to the Mill and give them money you had in the safe or something. That might work, but the police won't find any money in the SUV," I said. "What can we say caused them to leave empty handed so soon after they arrived?"

Myrtle was thinking. A smile formed on her face.

"They got a call that shook them up. They told us they'd kill us if we told anyone they were here and then left in a rush."

She had gained back her natural confidence. She stood up straight and looked at Marci. Marci nodded.

"Tom, thank you for all you have done. We can take it from here!"

22.

GERI flew me back to the farm. I thought it would be better if I were seen coming out of the forest. I asked GERI to let me out on the old forest road, far enough into the woods that we wouldn't be seen from the house. A few minutes later, I walked out of the forest and over to the barn. I unlocked the door and opened it wide so GERI could enter when he wanted to.

As he did, he told me that there was a vehicle with two men in it coming up the road toward us. I was standing by the barn when they drove up in an older blue pickup that had a canopy over the truck bed.

I didn't recognize the two men when they got out, but then I hadn't been in Tipton for fifteen years. I got the feeling that this wasn't a social call. They both topped six feet, outweighed me by a bit and appeared to be muscular under their soiled work clothes. The driver had thick, black hair cut short. The other man had sandy hair that was even shorter. They weren't smiling as they walked over to me. They didn't seem nervous, so much as uncertain about what they were doing.

"Should I come outside?" GERI asked, having seen the men through my implant.

"Yes," I said, "but don't do anything. I would like to avoid a rumor starting about strange, unexplainable things happening out here."

"Hello," I said congenially, when the two men stopped in front of me. "What can I do for you?"

The driver said, “Hi. My name is George Weaver. My friend here is Chuck Nethers. You met our wives the other day?”

Well, I hadn’t expected that. Where had I met their wives? I must have looked like I was wondering what he was talking about.

“It was at the Boarding House. Louisa, my wife, told me about it, and Chuck’s wife, Nina, told him.”

“Ah, thanks for explaining. Yes, we met. As long as we’re at it, what is Francis’ husband’s name?”

“Francis is divorced,” Chuck said. “She’s got a couple of kids and things are kind of tough for her.”

“Good to meet you,” I said, and shook their hands. I let them take the next step, whatever that might be.

“Louisa said that you had found some money out here,” George said.

I had no idea where this was going to go, but I thought I’d just listen. I nodded acknowledging that I had.

“Nina said you might be giving handouts to those in need in Tipton,” Chuck said.

I nodded again.

“We think that’d be a good thing for folks,” George said. “Like me and Chuck, a lot of people have had a hard time finding work since the Tipton Mill closed five years ago.”

I thought I’d get back into the conversation at this point.

“My name is Tom, by the way. I haven’t made the final decision, but I’m leaning that way. Your wives and I are going to talk about it tonight. I’d like to see what their proposal is.”

“Like I said, I think it would be a good idea,” George said. “Chuck and I were shift foreman at the Mill. We’re also both journeyman carpenters. We know that Simpson hadn’t done anything to this place for years. We thought you might be thinking about fixing it up. We'd like the job to help you do that if you were going in that direction. If you have a big project in mind, we know a few good men that would be glad for the work."

These were men who had worked hard since their youth. They had acquired skills. They wanted a job, not a "handout" as Chuck described what their wives were planning. I hadn't given any thought about the house and barn. Maybe it was time I did.

"I have some ideas for a new project," GERI chimed in over my implant.

"I'm not surprised," I sent back through my implant, "but you must also realize that having workers out here will make it difficult when it comes to keeping you a secret."

"We will work it out," GERI said, as if it wasn't a big deal.

George and Chuck had just made a proposal to me and I hadn't responded. My delay was rude. They were looking at me for what my reaction would be. They might be fascinated by the prospect of finding more money on the property, but they weren't here for that. They wanted a job if there was one.

"Thanks for coming out," I said. It sounded like a brush-off to them. It did to me too. I hadn't meant it that way.

"George, Chuck, I haven't given much thought about what to do with the place. It needs work that's for sure. I'd like to talk about it."

The effect was immediate. I was taking them seriously. They had asked, and I said let's talk. They had retained their dignity.

"Let's go into the barn. I'd like to ask you about something."

I imagined GERI might be wondering just what I planned to show them. I decided to let him wonder for a bit. I had some questions and I also wanted to take the opportunity to convince the people in town that there wasn't any more money on the property. When we were in the barn, I pointed to the floorboards and those up in the loft.

"These planks look like car-decking," I said, thinking that was a good place to start, "but look at how smoothly they have been milled."

"So that's where they went," George said.

When I looked like I could use an explanation, he continued.

"Years ago at the Mill we received this unusual order. Like you said, it was for the two-by-six tongue-and-groove product, but the order asked that they were finished so that all sides were smooth. That was difficult for us and expensive for the customer."

Chuck had wandered around looking at the barn. That seemed normal since I had begun asking about its construction.

"Hey! Tom is all of this equipment yours?"

George and I went back to where Chuck was. He had found a room toward the back of the barn. It was fifteen feet long and wide and full of power tools and hand tools for woodworking projects. There was dust on top of the sawdust on the floor. No one had been in the shop for some time. I hadn't gone that far into the barn to see that a separate workspace had been created.

"That explains something I found the other day," I said. "Let me show you."

We went back toward the front of the barn. I asked them to move the bales away from the trapdoor. I wasn't surprised they didn't see the trapdoor right away. I bent down and swept the dust away with my hands. I pushed the piece of wood hiding the ring. I pulled up on the ring, lifted the trapdoor and showed the *wine cellar* to my visitors. While they looked down into the chamber, I explained what I meant.

"Look at the cuts around the trapdoor and how the trapdoor was carefully beveled at the front so it would rise smoothly. Look at the siding and shelves and the fine workmanship in the way they were cut and assembled. I'm thinking that Simpson used that equipment back there to do this. You can climb down there if you like."

They did just as I suggested.

"We didn't supply this cedar," George said. "I see what you're saying about the workmanship."

Chuck looked under the trapdoor at the top edges of the chamber and said, "This is a concrete vault that's been lined with cedar. Is this where you found that money?"

Since I knew which money he was referring to I could answer truthfully.

"I looks like a good place to hide money, but I didn't find that money here. I found it under some floorboards in the house in Simpson's second-floor bedroom closet. I'll show you that if you'd like."

They came up out of the chamber eager to see where the money had been found. We closed the trapdoor and moved the bales back. I took them to the house.

On the way through, I could see them looking at possibilities for remodeling and other improvements. I took them upstairs and into Simpson's room. I showed them the boards. I let them lift them up and look around under the floor as much as they wanted. They found nothing there, nor had they found any money in the best place to hide it in the barn. I knew other people in town would know these facts soon.

We left the house and went over to where their pickup was parked. They told me about the ideas they had. GERI had already given me his idea for an additional building with an electronically operated garage door. We talked about their ideas,

GERI's addition and other possibilities. GERI had also asked me to tell them that I knew of another project they might be interested in and that I'd contact them about that at another time. We exchanged contact information. They left encouraged and armed with new information for the rumor mill.

23.

I went back to the barn and sat at my usual place on the bales over the trapdoor. I needed to get a more comfortable chair in place of the hay bales.

"What new project?" I asked.

"I am buying a building," GERI said. "I need some modifications done to it."

"You're what? You're buying a building?"

"Actually I am leasing it first," GERI said calmly. "It will take time for the purchase to close and I need immediate access to the building so I could begin making changes to it right away. By the way, I need you to sign the papers for me today. I've made the appointment for 2:00 p.m., but I'm sure the agent will be flexible on the timing. The property has been on the market for months."

"Wha…But…?"

Actually I didn't know what question to ask first. GERI's announcement surprised me. My friend from outer space had become a property developer.

"GERI, if you are actually purchasing the building, could you start by telling me where you got the money?"

"I invested the money we took from Travola's bank account."

"We were going to use that to help others."

"It still can be used for that purpose. I returned the money I used to the account after the value of my investments grew to a self-sustaining level."

"But we only took fifty-thousand out of Travola's account."

"That was sufficient to get me started."

"Wait! You would need to have a Social Security number to get an account with a brokerage firm."

"I have one. I also have a name and a history as far as government systems are concerned. I chose Gerald as a first name, so that if you referred to the friend you were helping as GERI it would seem natural."

I didn't want to ask how GERI became Gerald with a Social Security account and a history. I was fairly sure what GERI did to accomplish that.

"I chose Marshall for a last name. Since I am not from around here I thought you could use Mars as a mnemonic so you could remember it."

"How much have you accumulated so far, 'Gerald'?"

"Ten million and change," GERI said.

He was picking up the nuances of our American form of English quickly. I also could imagine how Gerald made that much money that fast, but I asked anyway.

"I started in commodities," GERI said, "but the turnaround was too slow. I found that currency trading suited my purposes better."

I hadn't thought of currency trading, but it was a natural for an intelligence like GERI. I also didn't have to ask about how he was dealing with taxes. I knew he was and that I wouldn't understand his answer.

"How much are you aiming for?"

"Ten million was my target," he said. "Now that I have attained that level, I have shifted the money to investments that do not require so much of my attention. That will allow me to focus on the property and my plans for it."

We took the money out of Travola's account last Friday, four days ago and two of those days were a weekend. Perhaps currency trading was a 24/7 activity. Four days to go from fifty thousand to ten million. Only GERI could do that.

"When did you arrange this property purchase?"

"I have been looking for the right property for several days. When I found this one, I contacted the agent on Saturday. The arrangement I suggested was unusual for her, but when I made a significant financial commitment to guarantee that I would purchase the property when that was possible, she was glad to accommodate my requirements."

"How did you contact her?"

"I sent her a text on her phone to begin the process. Then we have been exchanging emails. She sent me a contract which I edited and sent back to her. She agreed with the changes this morning. I told her that I would have a friend come in to sign the papers for me this afternoon. Can you do that for me?"

"GERI, why are you purchasing this property?" I asked. It seemed like a reasonable question.

"I can't tell you that," GERI said.

Apparently it was not a reasonable question. I would need some assurances before I would go along with this.

"What kind of property is it?"

"It is a large building on about thirty acres. It was built for the purpose of manufacturing custom furniture. There was insufficient capital left over after constructing the building so the business never got started. It was constructed three years ago but is essentially a new facility."

"GERI, I want to help you. I respect your right to your privacy. If you can't tell me what you are planning to use the building for, can you assure me that no harm will come from you doing whatever you'll be doing."

"I am sorry that we have to have this secret between us, Tom," he said. "I assure you that I am not doing anything that will harm others. I may be able to tell you about this sometime in the future, but until then it is absolutely necessary that you do not know what this is about."

I was very curious about what GERI was planning, but I had no reason to doubt his assurance, so I let it go.

"Alright, GERI. That's good enough for me. Now, what is the project you spoke of that might involve George and Chuck?"

"I will need to make changes to the building. If you think George is the right person, I would have him manage the project to make those changes. I would like you to work with him, but I hope it will not take too much of your time."

"What about the design for the changes, and the materials you'll need?"

"I have already designed the changes, made the drawings that George will need, and ordered the materials. The drawings have been delivered to the agent's office. You can pick them up when you sign the papers. Most of the material will be delivered tomorrow. There are some things that will take a few more days, but they should arrive in time to avoid any delays. If you and George could be there to receive the materials, we can set a time for the deliveries so that the materials can be put inside the building."

What could I say but, *yes* to everything GERI needed? GERI gave me the address of the agent and of the building that he was going to purchase. I called George.

"Hi, Tom," George said. "I didn't expect to hear from you so soon."

"My friend, Gerald Marshall, just told me that he's ready to begin. He is buying a building and wants someone to manage the project to make changes to it. I recommended you and he said yes. Are you interested?"

"Damn right I am!" George said. "I'll have to see the place and the plans, but if everything is as clear cut as you seem to think it is, I'm ready to start immediately. I know Chuck is as well. If we need more men, I'm sure I can line them up. Where's the building?"

"It's near the highway about halfway between Tipton and Bellingham."

"That sounds familiar," George said. "What's the address?"

I gave him the address.

"Wow! Your friend has bought himself one fine building. That building was built for a guy named Hopkins. I was on the project. Hopkins demanded high quality materials and solid construction. He watched every detail as we built the place. It was a pain in the ass, but he got what he wanted. It will be a pleasure working on it.

"Usually when you make changes to an existing building, you always find something you didn't count on that requires more work, money, and time to fix. We won't find anything like that with the Hopkins building."

I asked George to meet me at the site at three. GERI emailed me the letter that authorized me to sign for Gerald Marshall so the agent would have something to back up the transaction this afternoon. I drove back to the Boarding House to print the letter and get lunch if I was lucky. My days certainly seemed to be full since I arrived in Tipton a week and a half ago, and I was only halfway through this day.

24.

"How did the trip to South Carolina go?" Eleanor asked, as we sat down to lunch.

"There were complications," I said.

I told her what happened. She was upset about my having been connected to something that included criminals wanted for murder. I shared her concern. Then I mentioned talking with George Weaver and Chuck Nethers.

"George and Chuck? How did you bump into them?" she asked.

I was glad to change the subject. I told her why they came to the farm and how I thought it would squash the thinking that there is more money at the farm.

"George and Chuck, that's interesting. Their wives Louisa and Nina will be here tonight, along with Francis."

I asked her about Francis' situation.

"Her husband Dick wasn't a nice person," Eleanor said. "They were always fighting. When the Mill closed Dick lost his job and the only reason for sticking around. He left, and she got a divorce. It has been a struggle supporting herself and her two kids since then."

"I've been thinking about her situation since Chuck told me," I said. "If we go ahead with this, Francis will be giving support to others when she is in need herself. We need to do something to fix that."

"What do you have in mind?" Eleanor asked. "Everyone knows her difficulties, but we have to be careful about her feelings."

"I understand. I have a few ideas. There will be administrative work. I think Nina, Louisa and Francis should be paid for their efforts. That would help Francis. In addition I think she should also receive a check from the program."

"That sounds good so far, but when does Francis get the check before or after the program starts?"

"Exactly," I said. "Also, do we tell the other two, or keep it quiet? Will Francis accept the help?"

"Tom, this is up to Francis. We should call her before the meeting tonight. I'm her friend, but it wouldn't make sense for me to call her. I'm not part of it. You have to make the call."

Why does that not surprise me? Well, because in the first place it makes sense. It should be me. In the second place, it was only noon. I had two whole hours before I had to meet with the agent for *Gerald*. Whatever deity was arranging my days lately wouldn't have allowed me that much free time. So I called her.

"Hi Francis, this is Tom Williams."

"Hi Tom. What's up?"

"I wanted to talk with you about something before we all meet tonight. Do you have time this afternoon?"

"Sure. The kids are at school. Why don't you come over at one o'clock?"

"I'll be there."

Eleanor told me where Francis lived, and I arrived on time. It was a small home, but well maintained. Francis invited me in. She suggested coffee and we sat down with our coffee at the kitchen table.

"What did you want to talk to me about, Tom?"

I explained what I thought the situation was and my dilemma. She didn't say anything for a moment. Then it looked like she was going to cry.

Damn! Someone else should be doing this. I know it had to be me, but it looked like I had failed. She must have seen the concern on my face. She sat her cup down, reached over, and put her hand on mine.

"Thank you, Tom. I've been wondering about this from the beginning. I was glad to help put the program together, but I couldn't figure out how I was also going to be a recipient. You're coming here today, well, it's a great relief."

Whew! That opened the door for the next step.

"Francis, I don't know what the grants from the program will be. I imagine they will be in different amounts for different situations. This is what I believe your circumstance requires as a grant," I said, as I handed her the check for ten thousand dollars, which I had written out before I left the Boarding House.

She looked at it in disbelief. I know she thought she should refuse, but she also knew that she needed the money. She rose from the table, so I did too. She laid the check on the table and came over and gave me a hug.

She held onto me tightly, and with a bit of a sob in her voice, she whispered in my ear, "Thank you, Tom. Thank you!" She held me in the hug for a bit longer, pressing her body close to mine. It was like she didn't want to let me go. A moment passed. She sighed and stepped back and looked at me.

"You have brought new life to our town, Tom. You have already made a huge difference. Eleanor is a lucky woman."

We struggled a bit with our goodbyes. I left pondering what she had said and headed for the real estate agent's office.

I was scoring well on timeliness. I got to the office exactly at 2:00 p.m. The agent's office was at the end of a one-story strip of five offices. The building was relatively new and had a cedar shake roof. The wall with the office doors facing the parking lot had dark brick up the first three feet. The overall look was attractive for that type of building.

I was greeted by a young man sitting at the receptionist's desk. I told him that I had an appointment with Ms. Tolliver, and he led me to her office.

Ms. Tolliver got up, shook my hand, and invited me to sit down. She looked to be forty-five and was all business.

"This is an unusual arrangement, Mr. Williams, but nothing I haven't seen before. Your Mr. Marshall seems to be in a great hurry. Do you know what he is going to do and why he's in such a hurry?"

"No, Ms. Tolliver, I do not. He said he couldn't tell me what he was doing, but he assured me it was nothing illegal or harmful. I trust GERI thoroughly. Without knowing the details, I can tell you that he is highly creative and has invented several things since I've known him. He's probably working on another invention, and when he gets an idea, it drives him to act on it as soon as possible."

"Well, he has agreed to the contract before you, and has fronted me my commission on the purchase."

"That agrees with what he told me. He said that I only needed to give you this letter of authorization and sign."

I handed her the letter. She looked at it.

"This looks like it will work," she said.

I signed the lease agreement and the commitment to purchase at a later date. I asked her for the drawings. She handed me a three-foot long plastic tube.

"Does he always work this way, having someone else do the paperwork?"

"This is the first time he's asked me to do this, but I wouldn't be surprised if he has always worked this way. He is a bit of a recluse."

I stood up. She shook my hand and handed me the keys to the building. I met George at the building at 3:00 p.m. Chuck was with him again.

The building was rectangular in shape, eighty feet long and forty feet wide. Its light-green, metal walls were twenty feet high and there were small windows along the top of them. There was a door near the end of one of the long walls, which led into an office.

The three of us entered the office. It had a counter near the door and not much else. There was one table and four folding chairs on the other side of the counter. George, Chuck, and I went through the office and out into the main part of the building. Other than the space the office took up, the building floor was empty. There was a fifteen-foot wide roll up door at the end of the building where the office was, and a normal-sized door at the other end.

"Nothing new here," George said. "It looks the same as when we finished building it. Let's go into the office and see those drawings."

We went back into the office and I took the drawings out of the case and unrolled them on the table. It was a stack of twenty sheets of paper three feet top-to-bottom and four feet wide. George and Chuck looked them over, making approving noises as they did."

"Can you tell what Mr. Marshall wants to do?" I asked.

"Yes," George said. "The design and material specs are well laid out. Essentially he is building a large room in the center of the bay out there. He is also changing the large door for another type and reducing the opening. Then he has storage racks and bins along the walls. If the material is available, Chuck and I along with a couple of others can have this done in about three weeks."

"GERI will be happy to hear that," I said. "So do you want to do the job?"

"Absolutely!" George said. "What are we going to get paid, and how will that be done?"

"I don't think GERI has any idea how to structure that part of it. You will never meet GERI. He doesn't interact with people much. I'll make the payments to you, George, and you can pay the others. I'll be with you all the way in case there are complications. I suggest that you work up a bid. Add twenty percent for contingencies. Then I'll pay you some up front and weekly progress payments after that."

George and Chuck thought that would work just fine. We agreed to meet at the building tomorrow morning at 10:00 a.m. to start receiving the materials. I sent the time to GERI so he could schedule the deliveries. I locked up and we left.

I went back to the Boarding House and cleaned up. Eleanor and I sat down to the evening meal a little ahead of our usual schedule because of the meeting later. I told her about my day, and she shared some things about her writing.

"You've been a busy boy," Eleanor said. "How did Francis handle it?"

I told her how Francis reacted and asked her to keep tabs on how Francis was doing in case we need to give her another *grant*."

The meeting with Louisa, Nina and Francis went as I expected. They would find an office to work out of. They decided how much they should be paid. I told them that I would arrange for them to have signature authority to write checks on the account.

During the meeting Nina brought up Francis' situation and said we should give her the first grant. Francis didn't know what to say. She looked at me. I smiled back. I told the others that I would talk with Francis, and we would work something out. That satisfied their concern, and Francis was relieved.

When the women left, Eleanor brought out a bottle of exceptionally fine Port along with two elegant sherry glasses, and we talked some more.

I went up to my room later and I reflected on the day. I had moved around so fast and with so many people that I might be some tycoon making huge deals. The trouble with that comparison was that I didn't make any money. I was giving it away—A little over a million in the morning, ten thousand in the afternoon, signing somebody else's real estate deal, and donating several hundred thousand in the evening.

25.

"What are you going to do with your new building?" Eleanor asked.

We seemed to be having fun conversations at our breakfasts. It must have just hit her that part of what I said yesterday included buying and modifying a building. I wondered if she was getting ideas for her books from learning about what I was doing during the day. I asked her about that.

"Don't change the subject," she said, with a big smile on her face.

I guessed that the smile meant that she *was* getting some ideas for her books, but she wanted to steer us away from the topic by focusing on my escapades.

"The building is not mine. I'm just helping make the modifications that the new owner wants."

I didn't think I could evade the question about who the new owner was, but I thought it was worth a try.

"Who is the owner?" she asked.

"GERI."

The look on her face was hard to interpret. It seemed to be conveying several thoughts—surprise, incredulity, a little fear, a lot of *what the hell.* The last part showed mostly in her wide eyes.

"Uh, Tom, we need to talk about your *friend.* When you explained what he was the first time we talked about him, I got the impression that it was sort of an artificial intelligence running that thing you rode in. There's more isn't there?"

"Yes. GERI is a self-aware, cyber-based intelligence. He is a person, Eleanor, not a computer—a highly intelligent person. Have you heard the word 'singularity' in the context of artificial intelligence?"

"Yes," she said. "I think it means an artificial intelligence that is smarter than we are. Some people fear that we won't be able to control what it does, and that it would take over the world."

"GERI is that singularity, well not exactly. He is not from Earth. He doesn't want to take over the world, by the way."

"He told you that?"

"We discussed it. That's what he said."

"But he could?"

"I imagine. Let's talk about him and what he can do and leave off the 'take over the world' language. GERI has already connected himself to the world network. He can hack into any digital system without being noticed. It is true that he is in a vehicle that can move around very quickly, is undetectable, and can be invisible to our sight. That vehicle is not him. He is merely residing in it, because it was what he was in when he became self-aware."

"What does *he* want with a building?"

"He told me he couldn't tell me, but that I shouldn't worry about it."

"I don't find that as reassuring as you apparently do, but I have a more basic question. How did he buy it?"

I told her that he had created a name and history for himself. I gave her a sketch of his investment success. I provided more detail about the purchase and design for the changes in the building. I told her what I was doing in the project to help GERI.

"Tom, some of what GERI has done is illegal."

"That's true. It's also true that he is a person who is unable to function in this world unless he does some illegal things. He isn't abusing the power that he has. He is just doing what he needs to do. I'm just trying to help him find a way to live here if he wants to stay."

"Are you for real, Tom?"

I didn't know which aspect of me she might be referring to, or if she meant all of me. I thought the best strategy was to wait and see what she meant.

"You stood up to a dangerous criminal who wanted to take this house from me. You find money in your new property. You find who it belongs to and go through great efforts to return it and make sure they are safe. You are going to give the other wealth you found to needy people. You are the chosen friend of a superior intelligence, and you want to help him too. Are you really that self-less?"

"Hmmm. *Self* never came up, Eleanor. It never occurred to me to do those things any other way."

She got up out of her chair. I wasn't sure what she was going to do, but I thought I had better get up. She came up to me.

"I really like the person you are, Tom. I really like *you*."

She hugged me and put her head on my shoulder. I responded by hugging her. She felt so good in my arms. Still holding on to me she brought her head up. Her face was right next to mine. She leaned in and kissed me. It startled me at first. It took me an entire two seconds to get over that and to respond. I kissed her back. Her kiss wasn't one she would give to a brother. I wasn't acting like she was my sister either. We kept kissing for a long, beautiful time. We drew back to breathe and to look into each other's eyes. We both found what we were hoping for and kissed again, even more passionately.

We separated. She held on to my hands, and looked at me, smiling. After she had kissed me, her smile had an even more profound effect on me. I felt the need to sit down, but I resolved to stay standing and follow her lead. We hugged again and then sat down. Neither of us was sure what to say next. I tried to joke about it.

"Wow! Dessert with morning coffee."

It fell flat, but she smiled anyway.

"Tom, this is awkward for me," Eleanor said, "but I have to say this now, before I lose courage. Do you remember when we talked that night you checked in?"

"Yes," I said, breathlessly. I still hadn't regained the breath she took away by kissing me.

"We discussed the fact that neither of us had married," Eleanor said. "I said that I hadn't found the right person. I hadn't thought about it as clearly before, but I knew it at that moment. The reason it was so clear was because I learned at the same time who the right person was. It was you.

"We never dated or even said much to each other in school. I don't know how or when it happened, but way back then, my heart settled on you as the right person for me.

"I didn't know why I wasn't attracted to other men. I thought it was odd. I didn't know that I was waiting for you. If you hadn't come back, I might never have known the reason. Now I know."

Eleanor had just described my feelings and experience with other women at the same time she was telling me about her life. She was looking at me, concerned about my reaction to what she had just said. She had just bared her heart to me. Instead of responding, I was thinking.

"Eleanor, I liked you from afar when we were in school," I said. "I never followed up on those feelings. You must know how I feel about you. Every time you smile at me, I get warm all over and weak in the knees. When you explained how it has been for you, you were telling my story at the same time.

"You said it was awkward for you, Eleanor. I can see how it could be, but let's remove the awkwardness. I'm me, and you are you. We like each other. Nothing else matters."

She smiled, and then chuckled. She stood up and held out her hand. I stood up and gave her mine.

"Mr. Williams, in your short time boarding with us you've seen very little of my home. I'd like you to see the rest of it, starting with my bedroom."

26.

The beautiful time I spent with Eleanor was so wonderful I was late getting to GERI's building. George, Chuck and the first of the delivery trucks were waiting for me. Without a word of explanation, I unlocked the office door. George went to the roll-up door and opened it so the man in the truck could back it into the building.

One delivery truck after another came. George supervised the unloading. When material that wasn't needed in the remodeling project was delivered, George came up to me.

"I don't understand what these bags of ceramic pebbles are for."

"I have an idea that GERI will be using them for whatever he wants this building for."

After the ceramic pebbles, other items showed up including a supply of titanium and other elemental materials I didn't recognize. All George could do with these deliveries was to make sure they were stored in a place that didn't interfere with the remodeling project.

One item that was part of the remodel came in five-gallon cans, along with a special sprayer. It was to be sprayed over all interior surfaces of the new room that was being constructed. I looked at the bill of lading to learn what it was. It wasn't paint in the conventional sense. When sprayed on the interior of the room it would completely block all forms of electronic snooping.

"What is that for?" George asked.

I told him it was a special type of paint, that should be applied in two coats, and that the person doing the spraying needed to use the protective clothing provided and follow the instructions on the five-gallon containers.

I decided to leave when it appeared that George and Chuck had things well in hand. I gave George a duplicate set of keys that Ms. Tolliver had given me. I didn't want my tardiness to affect the timely completion of the remodel project. GERI seemed desperate to get started.

George stopped me as I was heading out.

"Are you sure the owner's name is Marshall and not Hopkins? All the materials going into the remodel are of the highest quality. The design, the drawings and the supporting documentation are extremely clear to the point of being meticulous in every detail. The County Building Inspector is going to love this."

"It's the way GERI does things, George."

"Is he going to show up, and look over our shoulder like Hopkins did?"

"No. He has every confidence that you will carry out his plan. You can talk to me if you have questions."

Actually I couldn't guarantee that GERI wouldn't show up. I just knew that George wouldn't know he was here if he did.

As I drove to the farm to get the precious metals to sell, I called Ahshid Massal, the gold dealer. I told him the amount of gold and silver I had to sell. I didn't mention the platinum. GERI had said he wanted to buy that from me as well as some of the gold and silver. I told GERI I would give it to him. He insisted that he pay for it.

"That's too much for me to handle by myself, Mr. Williams," Ahshid said.

"Do you know someone I can go to instead?"

"You misunderstand. What I meant was that I cannot buy that much for my own account. I can still be the one to help you. I can sell it for you."

"How will that work?"

"You bring me the gold and silver. I will find buyers. When it is sold, I will give you the money minus my commission."

"You said, 'buyers,' Ahshid. Why more than one?"

"The main reason is that selling this much gold or silver all in one transaction will draw unwanted attention. There will be questions I don't think you will want to have to answer. I will sell it in smaller amounts to, as the saying goes, 'stay below the radar.'"

I hesitated. He must have guessed the reason.

"There is nothing illegal in buying and selling gold in this country, Mr. Williams. It's just that transactions with large amounts are routinely investigated to be sure that the metal hasn't been smuggled or been handled in some other illegal way. I don't believe you have done that. If I thought you had I wouldn't work with you. You will be asked where you got it, and you don't know where it came from before you found it on your new property. That will raise more questions and stretch the investigation out."

"I see," I said. "Thank you for knowing what to do."

"My pleasure. No thanks are necessary. When you get the documentation of the transactions, you will see that I have been well compensated for my efforts."

We both laughed, but for different reasons. I was happy to have him keep me "below the radar." From what he was implying I would pay dearly for the service, but it was worth it.

GERI was in the barn when I arrived. I told him about the progress at the new building. I also told him the bid George had prepared and said I thought it was fair. He didn't question the bid. He transferred money to my account to cover the bid and thirty percent more just in case. He also transferred money for the precious metals he wanted to keep.

I asked if he wanted to go to the building with me later. He simply said, "No." I was also certain that when the remodel was done, I would not be allowed in.

All of this made me feel that this was the beginning of the end of our working together. I imagined he would come if I called, but once the building was done and his secret project could begin, I probably would see very little of him. He would stay in the building, working all day and night on whatever was driving him. I could tell he was already working on it. His responses were short, and the playfulness was absent.

I loaded the gold and silver into my SUV and took it to Ahshid. Then I went to the bank to set up the account for Louisa, Nina, and Francis to use.

What a day. It had an extraordinary beginning. I had run around and taken care of everything on my list and it was only 2:00 p.m. I didn't know what to do with the spare time that loomed before me. The deity managing my calendar helped me with my dilemma.

My phone rang and informed me the call was from North Carolina. I was still in the bank parking lot and thought that was a good place to take the call.

"Hello," I said.

"Is this Mr. Tom Williams?" a woman asked.

"Yes?"

"This is Detective Natalie Thompson with the Charlotte Police Department."

"What can I do for you, Detective?"

"Actually, Mr. Williams, I'm not sure. I'm working on a mystery and looking into anything that might help me solve it. You were in Darlynn, South Carolina recently, correct?"

"Yes, Ma'am. I flew into Charlotte on Sunday and drove to Darlynn on Monday morning."

"Would you mind telling me what drew you to travel across the country to a town that very few people on this planet know exists?"

I laughed. I could tell she was frustrated and didn't like adding one more mystery to the one she was already dealing with.

"Sorry for the laugh, Detective. When you describe my trip that way, it does sound funny. I went there to visit Mrs. Myrtle Blackwell."

"Why?"

"To deal with a matter that was of personal interest to Mrs. Blackwell. You'll have to ask Mrs. Blackwell for the details."

"She won't tell me why you were there. Can't you give me something?"

I knew I needed to give her something or the milk in her coffee was going to curdle.

"Detective, I will only say this. I found something. I learned that it belonged to Mrs. Blackwell. When I contacted her, she asked that I return it. I did. Please don't ask for any more information."

"So you just up and flew clean across the country on your own to deliver it. Why didn't you mail it?"

I didn't answer. She went on.

"While you were there, according to Deputy Dickerson of the Fairfield County Sheriff's Office, you calmly talked an armed fugitive into giving himself up. You also told Dickerson that you weren't a friend of the family, and that you had just met Mrs. Blackwell. Yet you knew the fugitive's name and situation. Can you explain that?"

"Detective I can explain that, but I think it's time you tell me why you called me."

She told me about finding the two criminals on Tuesday. It all played out as I had hoped and had created the mystery that was troubling her.

"Was Mrs. Blackwell or her granddaughter hurt in the robbery attempt?" I asked.

"No. That part turned out well. It's the rest, the mystery surrounding how I was able to apprehend those two criminals that has me stumped."

"I'm so glad to hear that nothing happened to them. But I don't understand why you are calling me about something that happened on Tuesday. I flew out of Charlotte Monday night."

"I know, but the unusualness of your trip had me intrigued. Now, can you tell me how you knew about Roberts?'

"When I agreed to visit Mrs. Blackwell, I had to investigate her and her family to see what I had gotten myself into. It was during that investigation that I learned about Roberts."

"How did you get that kind of information?"

I didn't answer.

She sighed and said, "Another mystery. Alright, you can keep your secrets. You are an interesting person, Mr. Williams, but that's not the same thing as a 'person of interest.' It's the persons of interest that I must focus on. Deputy Dickerson asked me to thank you again. That was a brave thing you did. I'll add my thanks. I appreciate what you did for a fellow law enforcement officer."

We ended the call. I had the feeling that she thought the call was a dead end, and that I wouldn't hear from her again. Maybe the book on Simpson's wrongdoing could finally be closed.

27.

I dropped by Francis' home on my way back to the Boarding House. I gave her the signature cards for the account they would be using. After writing numerous checks, they might wonder if they had drained the account. If they asked me, I'd tell them there was still money in the account. What they wouldn't know is that I would make sure that there always would be.

When I came into the Boarding House, I didn't see Eleanor. This was her time for writing, so I didn't bother her. I went up to my room and sat down at the small desk that was set before a window, which looked out on the backyard. It was cloudy, like yesterday. The calendar had switched from October to November overnight. The backyard and the weather hadn't noticed. I had. I would always remember the first of November as the day Eleanor and I had shared our feelings for each other.

What happens now? We would figure it out. This was Eleanor's home. She has a life here. I would not assume anything. I'd follow her lead

I had left the door open. Eleanor looked in as she walked by with an arm load of linens.

"Hello, Mr. Williams. You missed lunch. Dinner will be at the regular time."

"Thank you, Ms. Jorgenson. I won't miss dinner."

We smiled at our boarder banter. It was always fun. Today it was helpful in another way. We could use the space between host and boarder as a buffer until we figured out our next steps. Eleanor smiled warmly, and then continued on her way.

I didn't know what to do next. I had been running around addressing things that had come up since I had come back to Tipton with the simple plan of walking around in my newly purchased forest. I could go find Eleanor and offer my services as a handyman, but that would be the first step in changing my boarder status to something else. That would have to wait. I had a few hours before dinner. Wait! That sounds like free time. Something is going to happen to fix that problem.

My phone rang.

"Is this Mr. Tom Williams?"

"Yes."

"Glad I found you. My name is Ferguson Jenkins."

I've met several people that have two first names, like Bill James. This was the first time I've met a person with two last names.

"What can I do for you, Mr. Jenkins?"

"I need to talk with someone about a project I was given. My mysterious client provided your name."

I had no doubt who the mysterious client was.

"That's been happening lately. What's your client's name?"

"That's part of the problem. He didn't give us a name."

I contacted GERI through my implant.

"No name this time?" I asked.

"It seemed best this time. I apologize, Tom, but I've started several projects this way recently."

"Do they all have to do with your secret project?"

"Yes. I don't have time to make everything myself. I've approached experts in their field, like Mr. Jenkins, who are set up to do what I want."

"Got it." I said. I didn't bother to ask more questions. "No," was GERI's usual response.

"Mr. Williams, are you there?"

"Yes. I think I know who your client is. He is an extreme recluse. What can I do for you? Are you having difficulty producing what he wants?"

"No. We have already made what he wants. I'm calling to ask you to pick them up."

Jenkins was the CEO, founder, and chief scientist at Crystal Dynamics. He told me where it was on Eastlake in Seattle. It was in an area where a lot of high-tech, small businesses were. It would take me about ninety minutes to get there. If Jenkins didn't take too long, I should be able to fulfill my commitment and be back in time for dinner. I arrived a little earlier than I expected.

Crystal Dynamics was comprised of a small office building with two adjacent light-industrial, metal sided buildings. I went into the office and found Jenkins.

"Call me Ferg," he said, when I introduced myself.

He was holding a metal case which was two feet square and eight inches deep. He set it up on the counter and opened it. Inside, nestled in thick foam packing, were five clear spheres. Since this was a place that dealt with crystals, I guessed each was one complete and perfect crystal. What could GERI want these for?

"This is what the client asked us to make, and I would like to talk to you about them."

He closed the case, picked it up and beckoned me to follow him into his office. As we sat down at a small table, Ferg put the case on it and opened it again.

"Since you are in the crystal business," I said, "I'm going to guess those are crystals."

"They are crystals, Mr. Williams," Ferg said, "but unlike any other crystals on this planet. If I were to put a label on the spheres, each is a Dynamically Layered Organic Crystal Lattice. Something like this has been theorized, but it has remained in the theory stage because no one could imagine how to make them."

"How did you make them?"

"My client gave me the instructions. We have a chamber where we can control temperature and pressure. It has nozzles which can spray gasses into the chamber to form crystals. We watch the process with an electron microscope to see the molecule formation. Perfect crystals are comprised of the same molecules throughout the crystal. Defects come when a different molecule shows up in part of the crystal.

"Our client provided a list of the ingredients and at what temperature and pressure they should be added to the mix. He gave us the design for a polymer and when to introduce it as a vapor. We don't normally use polymers in making crystals.

"Our first few attempts at following his instructions were failures. When we learned to follow his instructions precisely, we saw a previously unimagined molecule forming which had an enormous capacity for bonding with its neighbors. As the temperature moderated and the pressure approached one atmosphere, the molecules came together in a spherical shape and ultimately produced what you see before you—an organic crystal containing molecules which are connected with each other via a total of ten to the thirtieth bonds."

I was beginning to get a vision for what they could be used for if someone had the advanced technology to accompany the spheres. Ferg confirmed what I was thinking.

"If we had technology to use these crystals as data storage devices, one of them could hold an unbelievable amount of data or could be the basis for uncountable numbers of parallel processing units. Since we don't have that technology, they are just beautiful, hundred-thousand-dollar crystal spheres."

"Thanks for the explanation, Ferg."

"I have a problem, Mr. Williams."

"What?"

"Once we finished making the spheres, all record of the process disappeared. We had the precise steps on our screens from a file the client provided. The steps were meticulous in their detail. The design of the polymer was extremely complicated. We were so caught up in our fascination with the new science we were seeing before us, we didn't think to make notes. When the fifth sphere was completed, after celebrating our accomplishment, we checked and found the file with all of its instructions was gone.

"Can you get that file for us? We'd be willing to pay you a tidy sum for it."

"No. I can imagine your disappointment, Ferg. There is nothing I can do. If the client didn't want you to have it that's the end of it."

"Who is this client? We have found no reference in the literature that anyone has come close to producing this result."

"As I said, he's reclusive and apparently enjoys working on his own."

"Have you met him?"

"Only recently, and our communications have been brief."

"Do you have access to his systems?"

"Ferg, I'm going to forget you asked that question. I don't like what you might be implying by asking it."

"I'm sorry. I'm just desperate to have the information in the file."

"You won't get it. My advice to you is to forget about the file. You have a head start on all your colleagues in this field.

You and your team surely remember parts of what you did. I suggest you try to reproduce the result. After all, you know it's possible, which is way different from pursuing something that may never work."

On the way home I worried a bit about the new technology that GERI was introducing by having others helping him with his secret project. When I got to the farm, I gave GERI the case. He used his manipulator arms to put it inside his cargo hold. I didn't bother asking GERI what the spheres would be used for.

I asked him about the technology-transfer concern. He said that he recognized the danger and was trying to minimize it by not leaving any details with those who help him. If Jenkins would have tried to copy the information onto his system, GERI said he would have deleted it.

We talked a little more, and then I left. There was a distance growing between us. I was saddened by it, but GERI had a right to his own life and pursuits.

28.

During the next two weeks there were several more instances of picking up packages for GERI's project. Then he said there wouldn't be any more. I was glad to hear it. The last scientist who produced something for GERI was angry. He had tried to make a copy GERI's file. Failing that, he spent hours typing the information into his own file. The next day, both files were gone. He was so mad he tried to beat the information out of me. I had size and skills he didn't, so he gave up early in the scuffle.

George and his team finished the remodel of GERI's building ahead of schedule. I went to the site to give George his final check and collect all the building keys. I gave him a twenty percent bonus for the early completion and encouraged him to share some of the bonus with his team. I asked him to see me later about a project on my farm and said we would need an architect. After he left I took the opportunity to look at the changed building. I was sure that I wouldn't be allowed in the building again until GERI was done with it.

They had done an excellent job on the remodel. The work was professionally done, and the building was clean. The roll-up door had been replaced by a single, large metal panel ten feet tall and wide. It would open electronically with a signal GERI would send. There was also a smaller three-foot square panel to the side which was four feet off the ground and opened onto a bench inside the building. The surface of the bench was made of roller bars with railings on the side. I imagined this was for small deliveries which could be put through the small panel and pushed along the rollers from outside. GERI could open the smaller door electronically allowing the delivery to be made without his being there to receive it.

The interior room, which the crew constructed in the middle of the bay, had two standard thirty-inch, interior doors. One door was set in each of the two walls that opened to the east and west ends of the bay. There was also a GERI-sized door which could operate electronically. The walls of the room went to the ceiling of the building. A GERI-sized metal panel that was installed in the roof could also be opened electronically. The plans called it a ventilation panel. I believed its real purpose was to allow GERI to enter or exit the room through the roof.

All the supplies for GERI's project were still in the open bay where they had been stored during the remodel. I hadn't visited the site for a while. I could see several items that hadn't been there before. There were several containers filled with isolated elements like phosphorus and sodium. A few of the elements were rare. I reined in my curiosity. If I were ever to know what this was all about, it would be sometime in the future, when GERI thought it was right to tell me.

I locked up the building and would be giving GERI all the keys later when I went to the farm. Today, I would be meeting the demolition crew. I decided the best thing to do with the house was to demolish it and leave no trace of it on the ground where it had stood. Even with all the contents gone and the windows and doors open, a feeling of Simpson was still there, and I didn't like it.

The barn was different. I would work with George to remodel it to serve as living quarters and office for me with a space for GERI. I would have the GERI-features added even though I wasn't sure he would be around. He would always be welcome and have a place in the barn if he wanted it.

I went into the barn when I arrived at the farm. The demolition company owner was scheduled to arrive at nine. I had twenty minutes or so to say goodbye to GERI.

"GERI?"

"Hi Tom," he said, as he became visible in front of me.

I could be mistaken, but he sounded sad. We both knew he would be at his remodeled building full time from now on. Perhaps he didn't like that anymore than I did.

"They've done a great job on the remodel," I said.

I took the keys out of my jacket pocket and put them on the bale of hay, still the only piece of furniture in the place.

"I'm going to miss you, Bud," I said.

"I know, Tom. I will also miss you."

"How long do you think it will be?"

"I do not have an answer for that question, Tom."

His manipulator arms came out. They scooped up the keys and took them inside. GERI went toward the fully opened barn doors. I would have hugged the big guy, but that didn't seem practical. He paused at the door and turned toward me.

"Goodbye, Tom," GERI said. With that he became invisible and left.

The barn felt empty and cold. I left and closed the doors and headed toward the house.

The demolition man had arrived in his pickup at the same time I arrived at the house. As he got out of the truck and came toward me, I could see he was smaller than I expected. My expectation was of a big, Paul Bunyan type, which didn't make any sense. It wasn't like he was going to tear the house down with his hands.

"Hi, Mr. Williams. I'm Barton Thicket. My friends call me Bart.

"Hi, Bart," I said as I shook his hand. "My friends call me Tom."

"Did you have an interest in saving any of the building materials for yourself?" Bart asked. "It makes a difference in how we approach the job."

"I do not want any of it," I said. "You are certainly welcome to have any of the materials."

"I'll consider that," Bart said. "Do you have any other guidelines we should keep in mind?"

"Yes," I said. "I want nothing left of the house, the foundation or anything around it. I want the ground graded to match the contour of this part of the property. I will have others do the final groundwork. Your job is to leave the ground as if no house were ever there."

Perhaps the intense feelings I had about the place came through, because he gave me a questioning look.

"Is there any problem with my specifications for the job, Bart?" I asked.

He regained a professional composure. "No, Tom your directions are very clear."

We discussed payments. He had a remote credit card reader. I paid him fifty percent, which was expected for a project like this. We could hear the large demolition machinery coming down the road as we finished the transaction.

"We should be done today, Tom, including the final grading," Bart said.

"That is good to hear," I said. "I'll take a look at it when you're done. If everything matches what we talked about, I'll give you a call and authorize you to charge my card for the balance."

"You can take a week or so to pay the rest, if you need to."

"If you do the work today. You should get paid today," I said. "I'll give you a call."

"Thanks, Tom," Bart said, with a big smile.

He walked to where his crew was approaching. I walked toward the forest. I missed GERI already. I needed the comforting sound of the wind dancing in the trees.

I did not make it very far down the path toward the woods. One of the trucks that came up with the demolition equipment didn't park with the others. It was an older pickup, faded green in color, and came up right to where I stood.

A tall man with long gray hair bound at the back of his neck got out of the pickup. He was wearing an outfit similar to mine—jeans, jacket and boots. It was his face that caught my attention. I would guess he was from the local tribe. Aspects of his face looked familiar. Then I got it. He looked a little like Nina Whitehorse Nethers. I liked the face.

"Mr. Williams," he said, as he came up. "My name is Silver Whitehorse. I think you know my niece, Nina."

"I do, Mr. Whitehorse. I was just thinking that there was a family resemblance. Good to meet you."

"Please call me Silver. Is it alright if I call you Tom?"

I nodded, and he went on.

"Tom, I was wondering about your plans for the place. It looks like you are erasing Simpson's house."

"That is exactly what I asked the crew to do."

"What about the barn?"

"I plan to keep it much as it is but remodel it so I could live and work there. What is your interest in my plans, Silver?" I asked congenially. I was curious, not threatened by his questions.

"I am primarily interested in your plans for the forest, though I am glad to have as much of Simpson's presence removed as possible. I did not enjoy talking with him, but I had to. He was bound to honor a long-standing agreement the tribe had regarding the forest. He was angry about it but didn't violate it."

"What is the agreement?" I asked.

"There is to be no logging in the forest or development on this ground. You will notice that the land on both sides has been logged. There are old-growth firs on the land you purchased, and other things that our tribe reveres. Over a hundred years ago the tribe made an agreement with the owner at the time—a covenant that would run with the land, binding all future owners. The covenant allows a house, a barn, and cultivation on the land that already has been cleared, but nothing else. Our tribal land runs along the back of your property. The land on the north and south of yours would be nice to have, but the forest on your land is the parcel of particular interest to the tribe."

"I do not intend to do anything that would violate that covenant, but I wasn't made aware of it when I purchased the land. It's odd that it didn't show up in the title search made at that time. I'll look into that, Silver. I'll find the covenant, and make sure it is visible in the future.

"I just thought of something even stronger, Silver. I will never sell this land, and I will put it in my will that the tribe gets this land when I die. Uh, that won't be for a while yet, though."

Silver smiled. "That's more than I expected, Tom. Thank you."

"You're welcome, Silver. I have had a feeling about this forest since I was a boy. It's the reason I bought it. I want to walk in it, listen to it, feel it, but do nothing that would change it."

"Are you sure you don't have some blood of my people running in your veins?"

"I might have. It would be an honor if I did," I said.

We looked each other in the eye, smiled and shook hands affirming our agreement to protect and honor the forest in a way that was far stronger than a covenant on a piece of paper.

29.

“Do you have time to walk in the forest this morning, Silver?” I asked.

“I do not. I would like a rain check though. I haven’t spent as much time among those old trees as I would like. I can tell you one thing you might find useful,” he said.

“What’s that?”

“This part of the forest is filled with underbrush which makes walking difficult. You see that large oak tree on the edge of the forest?”

“Yes.”

“There used to be a well-worn deer trail near there. If it’s still there that would be a good way to get into the forest. Always listen as you walk the trail. A mountain lion or a bear might also be using that trail.”

He smiled broadly as we shook hands again, and then he walked to his pickup and drove away.

I thought about our encounter as I walked toward the forest. I liked Silver. We made a connection right away. It was like our spirits had known each other for a long time, and like old friends were glad to see each other again. I think his spirit liked practical jokes, though. It was the way he smiled at my reaction to the possibility that I might bump into a mountain lion or bear on the trail.

Instead of heading toward the old road into the forest, which was full of brush, I took Silver’s advice and walked toward the oak tree a hundred feet south of the entrance to the road. As I walked along the edge of the forest, I could feel its life, and I could hear the wind in the trees.

When I arrived at the oak tree, I looked for bare spots at the base of the bushes, which might be the beginning of the track I was looking for. I found a promising one directly behind the oak. I stepped closer and parted the brush. Sure enough I could see the trail. It wasn't completely free of undergrowth, but there was a well-worn path on the ground that would be interesting to follow.

It started to rain. I was thinking about going ahead anyway, but then my phone rang. Distracted by my talk with Silver, I had forgotten to turn it off. I had several options to consider. I could answer the phone. I could ignore it. I could smash the phone with the melon-sized rock near my right foot and make a solemn promise to never buy another one while I buried its crushed remains at the foot of the oak tree. That last one was tempting.

I bent down and picked up the rock. Since the rain was increasing in intensity, I used the rock to mark the trail instead. I looked at my phone. I didn't recognize the number. I turned, walked back toward the barn, and answered the phone.

"Hello."

"Mr. Williams?"

"Yes."

"The organization I represent would like to talk with you about a technology that your name has been associated with."

I contacted GERI silently through my implant. "Are you listening to this?"

"Yes, Tom. I'm tracing the call and will investigate the individual when we learn his name."

"I probably will be getting more of these kinds of calls and some of these people will attempt to force me to give them what they want."

"I understand. I have prepared some things that will help."

"Thanks."

To the person on the phone I asked, "What is your name?"

"Fred Dillon."

"Got him," GERI said, via the implant. "He is a type of consultant. His most recent consultant fees were paid by a company called, Kudu Communications Technologies. Kudu's CEO, Charles Sorskia is a native of South Africa and has a history of questionable business practices. The company's offices are in Seattle."

"Thanks, GERI."

"Who are you representing?" I asked Fred over the phone.

"I can't tell you that at this point," Fred replied.

He seemed pleased with himself and practiced at protecting his clients. I decided to let him make his pitch.

"What technology are you referring to, Fred."

"The spherical crystal that was made for you by Crystal Dynamics."

"I guess the confidentiality agreement didn't mean much to Ferguson Jenkins," I said.

"He tried to honor it," Fred said. "In talking with a colleague at the firm I represent Jenkins let something about those crystals slip out and then quickly clammed up.

"My client asked me to investigate the matter. Ferg held out until I *persuaded* him to tell me all about the spheres, well almost all. Even with the pressure I applied he told me he didn't know how to make another one. Eventually I was convinced he was telling the truth. A man like Ferg doesn't hold up well in the kind of conversation we were having.

"He ended up giving me your name and number. He said you would be able to give me what I was looking for. I'd like to meet with you so you can do that."

The arrogant bastard was bragging about hurting Ferg, and thoroughly confident that he would get the information from me if we had the same kind of *conversation.*

"Gosh, Fred. It sounds like you were hard on Ferg. I wouldn't like that kind of conversation."

"The conversation with you wouldn't have to be that way if you give me what I want. So when can we meet?"

To GERI I said, "This guy isn't even trying to hide what he's willing to do to get the information about the crystals. I may be able to turn his violence back on him, but perhaps you have something else in mind"

"I do," GERI said.

"Whatever it is, how soon can you have it ready and how do I get it?"

"The two things I thought would be helpful are operational now. One is a portable energy field generator. It will create an energy barrier that will protect you. No one can get to you, but you can reach through it to disable your attacker. I've left the device in the barn, in the *wine cellar*.

"The other item is a security drone that can become invisible like I can. It will always hover quietly over you, and it will alert you to anyone approaching. It also can attack. Its weapon is like the one we used in South Carolina. It can be set on stun, but if things get worse, the weapon is capable of injuring or killing your opponents. The drone also has limited transport capability. It can lift a human or something else of that approximate weight and move it. That should probably be used at night because the human or package won't be invisible. It can move quickly, nearly as fast as I can. It is hovering over you right now. You can communicate with it through your implant as you do with me. It also will be my eyes and ears near you. It has an intelligence level equivalent to advanced Artificial Intelligences on this planet. Of course, the drone will respect your need for privacy as I do,"

"Thanks for looking out for me GERI."

"I put you in this position. It is my obligation to see that no harm comes to you, my friend."

"Mr. Williams, are you still there?" Dillon shouted through my phone."

"Yes. I was just thinking about your threats. I guess we should meet."

"Smart man."

We agreed to meet at seven p.m. at the barn. I thought it was better to meet at night and out of sight. He seemed to like that for his purposes as well. I could almost see him smiling. By the time we hung up, I was back at the barn.

I looked over and saw that the house was nearly down to the foundation. A large Caterpillar excavator with a demolition grapple was chewing the house into small pieces which would fit into waiting trucks. I saw Bart on the phone by his truck. I waved and went into the barn. I left the door open.

"Hello, Drone," I thought over my implant. I wanted to see if it picked up on thought the way that GERI did.

"Hello, Tom," it responded.

"Please come into the barn with me."

As soon as I had closed the door, the drone became visible floating three feet in front of me five feet off the barn floor. It was a dark blue sphere forty inches in diameter. There were a few lights blinking beneath its blue surface. There were no antennae, but those could be below the surface. There were no apparent arms, so I wondered how it carried things. As if it heard my question, a panel opened on each of its sides, and multi jointed arms extended pointing toward the floor. On the end of the arms there was a multi-fingered hand of sorts. Then the arms were quickly retracted and hidden inside the sphere again.

"May I call you Drone?" I asked.

"Drone works. What can I do for you?"

"Did you listen in on my last phone call?"

"Yes, GERI said you wanted your phone calls monitored. The human you were talking with sounds like a nasty piece of work."

Hmmm. GERI seems to have transferred his American English dictionary and his predilection for thriller novels to Drone.

"Yes, he is. Since I will meet him inside this barn would it be best for you to be inside with us?"

"Yes, Tom. I'll be in the rafters and will nail the bum if things get out of hand."

"But..."

"Don't worry. I am programmed to use the least amount of force to accomplish the objective. So when I said 'nail' him it was with that in mind."

"Thanks. It's time for me to learn about the defensive energy field that GERI made for me. He said he had placed it in the *wine cellar*. Do you know about it?"

"Yes, I can answer your questions."

I moved the bails aside, lifted the trapdoor and climbed down into the *wine cellar*. Inside on a top shelf was a small device about the size of a mobile phone only thicker. It was flat-black in color and there was nothing on its smooth, ceramic-like surface except for the hook on the back. Using the hook, I attached it to the front of my belt, climbed out of the cellar with a load of questions, and closed the trapdoor. Drone began providing answers before I asked the questions.

"First we need to personalize the field projector to you," Drone said. "Once that is done, you can communicate with it through your implant as you do with GERI and me."

Drone went through a series of beeps, and the field generator responded with lights flashing on the front side beneath the black surface.

"Please take the generator off your belt and hold it in front of you toward me," Drone said.

I did as he instructed.

"Say your name and put your thumb on the front surface."

I did, and was startled to hear, "Hi, Tom," through my implant.

"You are now a team," Drone said. "Most of the time the generator will respond to any incoming risk automatically, but it will accept your instructions. It would help if you named it."

"May I call you Bob?" I asked the field generator.

"Yes," Bob said.

I was so focused on the process of initializing Bob that I didn't notice that Drone had extended its grappling arms, picked up a three-foot length of two-by-four that was by the wall, and was swinging it at my head. Bob came to life. A rippling of the air in front of me was all I saw before the board stopped abruptly, five inches in front of my nose. I didn't feel anything. Perhaps Bob absorbed the energy from the impact.

"Yup, looks like it works," Drone said.

30.

"Damn! You could have warned me, Drone."

"I thought this was a better test," Drone said. "You may be attacked without warning, maybe even by someone you thought was a friend. You two, especially Bob, need to be ready for that."

"What if Bob hadn't responded in time?"

"I would have stopped the board before it hit you."

Thinking of videos showing the trouble people have in a zero-G environment, I couldn't imagine how a body with no firm connection to the Earth could have brought that swinging two-by-four to an abrupt stop. Hell, I couldn't even imagine how Drone's hovering body could have initiated the swing, or how it could hover in the first place.

I let the Drone's claims go without further explanation. I figured that if whoever made GERI knew how to do the hovering thing, they also might be able to manage the inertia and momentum things.

"Bob, are you okay?" I asked.

"Certainly, Drone's test was well within my mission parameters. I saw the attack coming long before the board came close to you. I tracked Drone's movements. I make no distinction between friend and foe. Everyone and everything around you are potential threats."

That raised a question in my mind.

"A speeding bullet fired from a long distance would only be 'around' me for an instant."

"An instant from the perspective of your sensory apparatus," Bob said. "For me that instant would provide more than sufficient time for detection, planning and response. I would be ready to stop the bullet long before it arrived."

"Thanks," I said. "What happens to the energy the incoming body is carrying? What happens to the bullet?"

"I absorb some of the energy," Bob said. "The bullet would bounce away, flattened somewhat by the impact, without making an impression on my surface. A fist would bounce off my surface as well, but it would likely be damaged from the encounter."

I spent more time learning about Bob. I found that even though Drone swung at my front, Bob had formed a field all around me. I asked him what would happen if I was driving my SUV when the attack came. He said the SUV might get damaged, but I wouldn't. I asked about the Boarding House. Bob answered that I would be personally protected if something happened. Drone answered the larger question about the Boarding House and those in it, namely Eleanor.

"I have the ability to put an energy field like Bob around the whole structure should that be required. If assailants are approaching the house, I will notify you. It may make more sense to take care of them individually, rather than putting a barrier over the house. By the way, when you are driving your vehicle, I will be hovering over it and should be able to deal with most attacks before there is a chance to damage you or your vehicle. I'll be in communication with you if I detect a threat. If there is no time for talking, I will just take care of it."

"Thank you, Drone and Bob. I feel well protected. There is a subtlety that we should factor into your responses. The technology behind your functionality is so advanced that any visible result from their use may lead to questions. We should try to make things look as natural to this world as we can."

"Understood," they both said at the same time.

We spent time working on that objective by going through several scenarios and possible ways to adjust their responses to make things look *natural.* I thought it was a useful exercise.

I was able to get back to the Boarding House in time to have lunch with Eleanor. Betty Saunders was there. Eleanor had asked Betty to come over so they could begin preparing for Thanksgiving.

The arrangement Eleanor and I made, that I would be the sole boarder, would end a week before Thanksgiving. Betty would be coming in during the day now and sharing our evening meal. There was the possibility of additional boarders. Eleanor had told me that relatives of local families often came to town to visit at Thanksgiving and Christmas. The situation for Eleanor and I was about to change.

I had continued to keep my room in the Boarding House. I always slept there, but Eleanor had taken me to her room a number of times since that first time two weeks ago. It had been wonderful. I didn't know how things would be with the coming changes. Eleanor would let me know of any changes to the Boarding House rules.

"How are things at the farm?" Betty asked, as we sat down for lunch. "I heard you found some money out there."

It was the first time I had actually seen Betty. I was amazed at how young she looked. If she was Jimmy Saunders mother, she must be nearly fifty. She didn't look it. She was five-foot seven, had brown hair, a pleasant smile and bright hazel eyes.

I told her about finding money in the house. It was no surprise that she knew about the program Nina, Louisa and

Francis were developing to distribute the money. I told her I was having the house demolished.

"Didn't you look for other places where there might be money?" she asked incredulously.

She said she would have carefully dismantled the house piece-by-piece to make sure there wasn't any more money stashed in there somewhere. I understood the sentiment. What she didn't know was that I had found another stash of money. That had given me the confidence that Simpson hadn't used the house as a place for more hiding places.

After lunch I went to my room. They needed to talk about Thanksgiving. I needed to think about how I was going to handle Fred Dillon. With all the possible variables, by the time I left for the farm all I had come up with was *carefully.*

All the demolition equipment and trucks were gone. There was one car there with a man in it. I assumed it was Fred Dillon. I parked and went over to where the house had been. I couldn't tell that there had ever been a house there. Perfect. I called Bart, thanked him and told him to go ahead and charge my card for the balance.

I heard a car door open and close behind me, and footsteps approaching. I turned and saw the man I assumed was Fred coming my way. He was five-foot ten. He had a muscular build beneath his windbreaker but didn't look menacing. He stopped three feet from me and held out his hand for me to shake.

"Mr. Williams?"

I nodded but didn't shake his hand. It remained in the air before us for a moment longer, and then Fred let it drop.

"Let's go to the barn," I said, and began walking in that direction. Fred followed.

I opened the door. The motion sensor light switch I had installed brought the overhead lights on as we entered. They were a little too bright—something to change later, should I survive the encounter with Fred. With only bales of hay to sit on, standing seemed the right thing to do. This wasn't a social call after all. We stood five feet apart facing each other.

"Do you have the information that I asked for?" Fred asked without preamble. "You aren't carrying anything."

His words by themselves were not threatening. The manner with which he spoke them, the apparent eagerness for action that could be seen in his eyes and the stance of his body were.

"No."

"That's unfortunate," Fred said. "Can you get it for me?"

"Fred, I agreed to meet with you because I was sure that it would be the only way to stop you. I will not give you any information. Please don't pursue the matter any further."

"Since my client won't stop until he gets what he wants I must keep on until I get it for him. Now let's see if we can change your mind."

He stepped forward. I held up my hand.

"I know your client is Charles Sorskia. He will not get the information. If I have to, I will contact him and make him aware of the futility of his efforts."

Fred stopped. With a questioning look on his face he said, "How could you know that?"

"Fred, unfortunately I know all about you and your client. I know where you live. I have your bank account numbers and access information. I know the business practices that Sorskia has used to become successful. I know about your service record and the facts behind your dishonorable discharge. I know about some of your past clients and the work you have done for them. I would rather not have learned any of it but thought it prudent to know who I was dealing with."

Fred's confidence was shaken, but my revelations apparently were not going to stop him from trying to get the information. He clenched his jaw and took another step forward. I held up my hand one more time.

"Fred, stop. Do you really believe that I would have invited you out here without preparing myself? You made it clear that if I didn't give you the information you would use violence to change my mind."

My second speech didn't deter Fred either. I had also learned that Fred's hand-to-hand combat training was at about the same level as mine. My advantage was that he didn't know about my background. That was apparent when he stepped forward and attempted to grab my jacket. I grabbed his hand and twisted his wrist. He got out of my grip and stepped back.

He came forward again and tried a few punches, all of which I deflected. He backed up and looked at me obviously wondering how I had done that.

"Fred, please stop before you get hurt. Go tell your client to forget about this."

"He won't give up," Fred said. "Neither will I."

He reached inside his jacket and pulled out a gun. Not being familiar with any kind of gun, my only assessment was that it was sleek and deadly looking.

"Put that away, Fred. Unless you shoot right away, you have lost any advantage the weapon might have given you."

He got a what-is-this-guy-talking-about look on his face. He looked at his gun, at me, and back at his gun.

"Huh?"

I leapt forward and grabbed the gun. It went off as I twisted it out of his hand. I didn't have to worry about the bullet. I knew Bob would take care of it. I stepped back with Fred's gun in my hand.

“See how dumb it was to bring a gun into this, Fred? I could use it to shoot you if I wanted to.”

I tossed it to the floor ten feet behind me. Fred was confused, frustrated, and looked like he was getting angry. Confusion, frustration, and anger do not usually lead to rational thought. Fred proved it. He tried to get past me to retrieve his weapon. He didn’t make it. I tripped him and put him on the floor with his face in the dust and stray stalks of hay. I quickly asked Drone to stun him. I thought the fall was good cover for becoming unconscious. I hoped that Fred would remember that he had fallen and guess that the fall had knocked him out.

Now what?

31.

Now what indeed! I was making it up as I went along. I felt good about what we had accomplished so far. Now what should I do with a one-hundred-ninety-pound, unconscious man?

Gloves! If I didn't put gloves on right away, I'd start doing things, and forget where my hands had been, and leave fingerprints. So I put on a pair of the vinyl gloves I found useful during my time in South Carolina. Then I went over and picked up Fred's gun. I wiped off all surfaces with a cloth. Then I put it into Fred's right hand to imprint his fingerprints in the right places. I placed it in his shoulder holster.

"Drone, do we know where Sorskia lives?"

"Yes."

I thought it would be a good idea to drop Fred at Sorskia's front door. I hadn't worked out how to get him there. I could have Drone air lift Fred there, but then what would I do with Fred's car? I saw it when I came in. It was a new Toyota Avalon. I could drive it, but I might leave some evidence of my presence. Not good.

Then I remembered an article I had read ten years ago. It had reported that cars could be hacked, even those which weren't built to be self-driving cars. Since electronics controlled more things in newer cars, Fred's Avalon would be very hackable. Also, I might have the world's second-best hacker floating in the air above me—GERI being number one.

"Drone can you drive Fred's car?"

Instead of answering, I heard the car start up outside.

"If you'll open the barn doors," Drone said, "I'll drive it in."

Drone carefully parked the car far enough inside the barn so I could close the doors again. I opened the driver's door and looked over at Fred's body lying face down on the floor wondering about the best way to get him behind the wheel. Drone had been thinking about the same thing.

"If you flip his body over and raise him to a sitting position," Drone said, "I can put my arms under his arms at the shoulder and lift him that way, while you pick up his feet. Then you can guide his feet to the floor of the car and slide the rest of him onto the driver's seat."

It went more smoothly than I thought it would have. After we had him in place, I put the seat belt on to hold him there. His head slumped forward. I reclined the driver's seat back to help keep that from happening and closed the car door.

"I have mapped out the best route to deliver Mr. Dillon to Mr. Sorskia's residence. I will need to stay with the car to guide it successfully. I cannot do that because my programming requires that I stay with you at all times," Drone said.

"Would your programming allow you to guide Dillon's car if I were following a mile behind you in my SUV? I would like to stay far enough behind you so that it won't appear that I'm following you if someone looks at satellite recordings of the route of Dillon's car."

Drone said that would work and loaded the route into my SUV's mapping software.

"By the way, do you know how to drive?" I asked. "I mean do you know the rules of the road—stopping, signaling and the rest?"

"I have downloaded the Washington State driver's manual. I will use it as a guideline and adjust to circumstances as they arise."

"Sounds like that will work," I said.

I was nervous about it, but it needed to be this way. I opened the barn doors. After Drone backed the car out, I closed the barn doors from the inside. I waited five minutes before I left the barn. I got into my SUV and followed the mapped route. Through my implant I could see the Avalon as Drone was guiding it down the road. I looked at it occasionally while my primary focus was on my own driving.

Drone was making all the right choices. He stopped at stop signs and lights while we were on secondary roads. When he went south on I-5 he stayed to the right and signaled when he changed lanes. He took I-405 south to Bellevue and then went east on SR 520. Sorskia lived in an exclusive, gated community near Redmond. I wasn't sure what we would do when we arrived at the gate.

I shouldn't have worried about the drive or the gate. Drone was a better driver than I was. He arrived at the gate in two hours. Drone connected with the gate security and opened it. It surprised the guard in the gate house. He came running out waving at the car to stop. When the car kept going, the guard hopped into his security vehicle and raced after the unwelcome newcomer with his car's lights flashing. Drone paid no attention.

I didn't drive near. I parked a mile away and followed events through Drone's "eyes." As we had previously arranged, Drone sent a text message to Sorskia. The message said that his package had arrived. It also told him to stop his investigation, and that he would be watched to make sure he complied. Right after the message was sent Drone drove the car into Sorskia's driveway. He stopped the car, turned off the engine, and started the car alarm blaring.

Staying invisible, Drone came down closer to the surface. Looking in the side window of the car, we could see Dillon beginning to regain consciousness. The guard vehicle stopped in front of the house, and the guard ran up to Dillon's car. Sorskia came racing out of the house. He nearly tripped because he was trying to read the text message at the same time.

We had affixed a micro-transmitter to Dillon's skin, so we had the audio version of the chaos on the ground. Sorskia tried to calm the guard saying it was okay. The guard wasn't convinced. When Dillon got out of the car, Sorskia tried to ask him what had happened and why he was in his driveway with the car alarm going off, but the alarm made it impossible.

"Turn that damn alarm off!" Sorskia demanded.

Things were easier to follow after that. Sorskia apologized to the guard for not alerting him that his friend would be visiting and for his drunken condition. He said he didn't know how the gate had opened letting his friend in. The guard wasn't satisfied. He said he would report the incident to the community council and went away. Sorskia growled and turned toward Dillon.

Sorskia grabbed Dillon by the arm and dragged him toward the house. Before he got there, Drone was able to get close enough to affix a transmitter to Sorskia's neck as we had with Dillon's by shooting the transmitter with a high-speed air pulse. Sorskia swatted at his neck as if he were swatting at a mosquito.

After they entered the house they sat down in the den. Staying invisible Drone hovered outside the window. Dillon tried to explain what had happened. Sorskia was so angry he barely listened. He shouted at Dillon, asking why he had driven to Sorskia's house and set off the car alarm. He didn't believe Dillon's story about being unconscious. He told Dillon to start over at the beginning.

Dillon's version didn't match what actually happened, but it ended the same way. He was unconscious at the end.

"There's something odd about this whole thing," Sorskia said.

He showed Dillon the text message, and then cursed some more. Dillon stayed quiet, probably trying to figure out what was going on.

"I'll tell you one thing," Sorskia said. "They won't stop me! This makes me want the crystals even more. We'll just have to come up with some other approach."

His phone alerted him that there was another message waiting. Sorskia looked at Dillon and at his phone, seemingly reluctant to see what the message was. Finally he opened the message.

The message said, "We can stop you and we will. If you try another approach as you just suggested, that also will be stopped. There will be repercussions that you won't like. Please move on to something else. As you can see, you are being monitored."

Sorskia threw his phone to the floor as if it were on fire. He looked around desperately, trying to see who was listening in on his conversation with Dillon. There was no one there and nothing to be seen.

We left them wondering what had happened to them. Drone followed me back to Tipton, hovering above me at an altitude of one thousand feet. On the way I asked Drone to continue to monitor Sorskia and Dillon, but only alert me if it was obvious that they had disregarded our warning and were planning to come after me again.

It was nearly midnight when I parked in front of the Boarding House. As I went in, I realized that there were two additions to my entourage. Drone would hover above the house, but Bob would be coming in with me. If I told my host, I wondered if she would raise the rent.

32.

I found out what Eleanor thought about Bob in the morning at breakfast. That was one of the few times that Eleanor and I had time by ourselves, now that Betty was coming in during the day. Even that would change when there were additional boarders.

Bob didn't have an audio capability. He communicated with me only silently through my implant. I mentioned that when I explained to Eleanor about the latest complication in my life.

"So Bob is an *imaginary friend* then?" Eleanor asked, smiling.

What could Bob be to Eleanor but an "imaginary friend"? "My friend" as Eleanor called GERI, had moved out to his new building. In his place he gave me Drone and Bob.

"Why? GERI wasn't monitoring you that closely before, was he?"

I had to tell her everything. My presence might bring trouble. So I described the projects that GERI had outsourced and the kind of problems they might bring. I downplayed the danger inherent in the previous night's events. She read between the lines.

"Tom, this does not sound good," Eleanor said.

I wanted to talk about how the addition of Betty and possible new boarders were going to affect things between us.

My news needed to be discussed instead. It was more imminent and possibly dangerous.

"I know. It pains me to suggest this, but it's time I found other lodgings. If I'm not here, the danger won't affect you. It also might be the right thing to do because Thanksgiving is coming, and you will have more boarders to deal with. Our agreement about me being the only boarder ends next week anyway."

The look she gave me matched the way I was feeling. Her look seemed to ask, "What about us?"

I laid my hand on hers.

"This doesn't change how I feel about you, Eleanor. That will never change. I just don't want the issues I'm facing to hurt you in any way."

She nodded.

"Tom, I still want to be with you sometimes, like the times we've had."

I was not surprised, but I was glad to hear her say it.

"Me too, Eleanor. We'll find a way. Besides, I don't think this will last all that long. I have a feeling that whatever is driving GERI to work so hard on this will happen soon. I'm worried that I might lose him because of what he is preparing for. That would be sad, but not as important as what we have together. I don't want GERI's actions to affect us, especially you, in any way."

I told her that I would move into the Days Inn a few miles away. I said that if anyone inquired about me, she should give them my new location and not appear concerned at all. She said she could do that.

We spent a little more time talking. Since Betty was about to arrive. I went to my room, got my things, and left. I drove to the hotel and rented a suite there. I let them know that I might be staying a while.

Not rooming at the Boarding House also meant not eating there. Eleanor would probably be fine if I took my meals there, but that would just draw attention to the place, and I wanted to avoid that.

I decided to avoid the questions I would get if I went to Mel's. So after settling into my room, I got a cup of soup at the coffee shop next to the hotel. The soup was good, but they weren't open after lunch, so I would have to go elsewhere for the evening meal. I paid the check and walked back toward the hotel. My phone rang on the way. I answered and kept walking.

It was Eleanor

"Francis called an hour after you left," Eleanor said. "She wanted to know if everything was alright between us because you had moved out. I told her that you thought that your business pursuits would be better handled if you were operating from a hotel. I also mentioned that I needed the room for holiday guests.

"I wasn't surprised by the call. It was easy to see that she's attracted to you. She was happy that everything was alright between us. She asked me if it was alright if she had lunch with you some time. I said I wouldn't mind."

I didn't say anything. I hadn't thought of Francis in that way.

"Don't be so surprised, Tom," Eleanor said. "You're a caring, thoughtful person, and a handsome, single man. Women are attracted to you. I wouldn't be surprised if I get a similar question from Betty."

"About Betty, I was going to ask you how Betty Saunders looks so young if she is Jimmy's mother."

“That’s simple, Tom,” Eleanor said. “She isn’t Jimmy’s mother. She married Saunders when she was about twenty. At the time Jimmy was about fifteen. So Betty is only a few years older than you and I.”

“Thanks for the heads up, Eleanor.”

“You’ll be fine, Tom. We’ll be fine. Just be yourself.”

I drove out to the farm. I had asked George to meet me there with an architect he thought would be good for the barn remodel. When I described what I wanted, I found that they were way ahead of me.

The barn would be thoroughly cleaned. A new roof and windows would be added. It would have plumbing and wiring for a combination home and office. The loft would be designed as an open bedroom and office. The woodworking room would be walled off with doors to the interior and outside. An oversized garage would be added with its garage doors facing away from the road.

George and the architect accepted the spaces and openings I was making for GERI on the ground floor without asking any questions. I didn’t know if GERI would still be around. I wanted to prepare for that possibility. He would always be welcome.

When they left I checked in with GERI. I knew he was busy but could probably multi-task.

“Did Drone tell you about the events last week?”

“It did not need to, Tom. Though I am abiding elsewhere, I have never left you alone. I am constantly monitoring the input from your implant. I also am linked to Drone and Bob, and I monitor the network in general for anything related to you.”

In another circumstance with a different person I might have objected to the invasion of my privacy. In my circumstance I welcomed GERI’s oversight.

“Thanks, Pal,” I said. “How are things with you?”

"Things are not progressing as quickly as I wish. Other than that assessment, you know I cannot say more."

I didn't comment. When GERI stated a fact that was that.

"Tom, I think the projects I have asked you to get involved with have attracted the attention of your government. I believe someone will be contacting you soon. I will help where needed if you are contacted, as will Drone and Bob."

"My life has become complicated in another way, GERI. As you have probably surmised, Eleanor is my friend. You have made provisions for my safety. Is there something that you can do to at least monitor Eleanor?"

"I can make a drone to monitor her. I will link them with your Drone which can let you know if something is not right."

"Thanks, GERI. I had better let you get back to your project."

"Thank you for understanding what I am doing, Tom."

I drove back toward the hotel. Ahshid called and said he had sold all the gold and silver without any undue attention being paid to the transactions. My share was seven-hundred thousand. His was one-hundred thousand.

He laughed when I didn't say anything. I'm sure he thought it was because I thought it was too much. I didn't say anything, because I was fine with his cut, and was happy to have the gold and silver converted to dollars.

I picked up the check from Ahshid and went to the bank. Cynthia saw me come in and rose to help me with my deposit. She smiled as she told me how much she appreciated my business. Cynthia was wearing a cream-colored cashmere V-neck sweater tucked into dark gray slacks. The combination highlighted her womanly figure. I was sure all the attention I was getting was because of the business I was bringing to her branch. I hoped *she* didn't ask me out to lunch.

33.

I was in the bank parking lot after making the deposit and had just fastened my seat belt when my phone rang.

"Hello,"

"Is this Mr. Tom Williams?"

"Yes, who is this please?"

"My name is Derek Mathews. I'm with the U.S. government. I'd like to meet with you."

"What part of the U.S. government are you with?"

"I'll explain when we meet."

"When did you want to meet?"

"I'm in your hotel lobby. We can meet when you arrive."

"Fine. I'll be there shortly."

I called Eleanor. She said a man came looking for me and she said that I had checked out and that I had rented a room at the Days Inn. That all sounded fine. So far the U.S. government light was not shining on Eleanor.

I walked into the lobby and Mr. Mathews was sitting near the door. He rose to greet me, apparently knowing what I looked like. Mathews was wearing a nondescript gray suit that did not fit him well, a white shirt, blue tie and black shoes. He was five-foot eleven and weighed over two-hundred pounds. The left side of his suit jacket bulged out indicating a possible holster and gun.

"Mathews works for DARPA," GERI sent through my implant. "His title is Program Manager. It's a generic title that apparently covers many types of activities."

My experience with the Defense Advanced Research Projects Agency was mostly with scientists and other academics. Mathews looked more like a bodyguard than an academic.

"Thanks, GERI. Please record everything. We shouldn't rely solely on the security cameras here in the hotel. We will want a recording of our own."

"Mr. Williams, I'm Mathews. I'm with DARPA. From your time in the Air Force you probably have some idea what our agency does."

"Yes. May I see your identification, Mr. Mathews?"

He brought out his photo ID confirming what GERI had said.

"Thank you. What would you like to talk about?"

"Is there somewhere we could sit down?"

We went into the small room off the lobby, which had tables and chairs that were used to serve a light breakfast. It was empty at this time of the day. We sat down at a table away from the windows and where the security camera could see us clearly. I had already asked my question, so I waited for Mathews to begin.

"Your name has been associated with some interesting technology, Mr. Williams. DARPA would like to know more."

I waited. It was a statement, not a question.

"Mr. Williams, can you tell me more about the crystals that were made for a Mr. Marshall by Crystal Dynamics?" Mathews asked.

"No."

"What do you mean, 'No'?"

"It is my answer to your question. You asked if I could tell you about the crystals. I assumed you meant more than that Crystal Dynamics made them. I don't know any more than that."

"Oh. Okay, can you tell me where Mr. Marshall is?"

"No."

"You don't know, or you won't tell me?"

"I don't know where he is."

"Mr. Williams, you aren't being very cooperative."

"I disagree. I've answered your questions as well as I can."

"Mr. Marshall recently purchased a building which you signed for. I understand you managed the remodel of that building."

"Yes."

"Is Mr. Marshall at that building?"

"I don't know."

"Can we go look to see if he is there?"

"Of course. I'll give you the address."

"I have the address. I was expecting you to accompany me when I went there."

"Why would you expect that?"

"I assume you have access to the building, so even if Mr. Marshall wasn't there we could go in and look around."

"I don't have access to the building. I have no keys. If I did have a key, I have no authority to enter the property and 'looking around' would not be right."

"But you were there. You remodeled the building. Why don't you have any keys?"

"It isn't my building. Mr. Marshall told me to turn over all the keys to him."

"You don't find that unusual?"

"No. What I do find unusual is the conversation we are having. If there isn't anything else, I will leave now."

I got up to leave. Mathews grabbed my arm and tried to pull me back down in my chair. His hand slipped off my arm as if it were made of glass.

"I'm not done, Williams. Sit down."

I looked at him in disbelief.

"Who do you think you are? I answered your questions. We're done."

"No we are not. Now sit down."

"Or what?"

"Or I'll make you sit down."

"I feel I must warn you in advance, Mathews, that won't work. So what other consequence do you have in mind? Are you going to pull a gun and try to make me sit down?"

"If I have to. I'm with the U.S. Federal Government, with DARPA which means national security. I'll do what I have to do to get the answers I need."

"You don't really have a gun, do you?"

He pulled a gun out of his shoulder holster and pointed it at me.

"Now sit down, Williams."

I laughed.

"So here we are, in a public lobby and what, you're going to shoot me?"

He was getting angrier by the moment.

"No, but I can force you to come with me to a place where shooting won't be so public."

I laughed again.

"You have just placed yourself in an untenable position, Mr. Mathews. You have made a threat that you cannot carry out. I'm not intimidated by your gun, so I won't be going anywhere with you. I think you should re-read the book on successful information gathering techniques."

He looked like he was going to follow through with his threat. Instead he told me that I would hear from him again.

"I have a recording of our meeting, Mr. Mathews. When I send it to your bosses, I'll let them know that I don't know anything, and more threats won't be able to change that. If the next step in this DARPA information gathering exercise is abduction by some black-ops squad, please know that would fail too. I'd like to say it has been nice to meet you, Mr. Mathews, but it hasn't."

It was clear that Mathews was angry as he left.

I followed him to the door so I could get the license number of his car. Then I went over to the counter where the hotel staff member was standing open-mouthed. She was a middle-aged woman whose name was Silvia according to her name tag.

"Did you see what just happened?"

"Yes, I did," she said.

"I would like a copy of the security camera footage for the duration of that meeting."

"I don't think I can do that."

"Do you need the manager's approval?"

"Probably, but it's not that. I just don't know how."

"That bully may soon realize that he just performed a criminal act on video and may storm back in here demanding the security footage, saying it was a matter of national security. Let's not let him get away with that. I think I can make a copy if you'll let me. You will still have the original."

She nodded. Silvia looked like she was in shock. She took me to their security monitoring system. It was a simple system recording on DVD's. I found the one recording the camera in the breakfast room. I popped the DVD out and quickly put a blank one in so the record would continue, almost uninterrupted. I found a computer in the room that had a DVD drive. I transferred the entire recording on the DVD including the part I was interested onto a USB drive. I also copied the recording to the computer that I was using. It was unlikely that anyone would think to look there to erase it. If they did, they did. I couldn't do anything about that.

I told Silvia what I had done, so she could tell the manager when she reported the incident. I suggested that she call her manager right away, and then put the DVD in the rack where daily records were kept. I told her I would be going to my room and gave her the room number. Then I helped her to a chair where she could sit down and call her manager.

I went to my room, started my laptop up and inserted the USB drive. GERI copied the recording from my computer. He gave me a copy of the audio portion that he had recorded.

"GERI, I think we should get out in front of this. We should send these recordings to Mathew's bosses with a note briefly saying what they are. I think that I should also send it to the Sheriff's office. I don't have any idea how to get it to his bosses. Can you do that?"

"I have sent it. Tom, they seem to be the kind of organization which will try to get some leverage on you to force you to do what they want."

"I agree. Please monitor all my records. Do not allow any changes to existing records. Also watch out for new fake records, like criminal activity for example. They may try to frame me for something. They may think that if they create a record like that, I'll believe that they can make the false accusation stick. Please keep an eye on Mathews. He may act without his superior's sanction. Also, please start monitoring Eleanor right away."

"I have begun all that you have asked," GERI said. "The new monitor is in place above Eleanor's location."

"Thanks, GERI. I hope this isn't taking too much time away from your project."

"Don't worry," GERI said. "It isn't affecting my progress."

"It's unbelievable that the U.S. government would do this sort of thing under the name of national security," I said.

Drone said, "I put a transmitter on Mathews as he left the building. It will also serve to locate him at all times."

"Thanks, Drone!"

"Bob, that was a good way to keep Mathews from being able to get a grip on my arm. He was confused why he couldn't, but you gave away nothing. Good job!"

"Thanks, Boss," Bob answered.

"The only other thing I can think of that they might try is to freeze my bank accounts. Can you stop them from doing that, GERI?"

"Yes, but in case I can't stop them, I have set up a new bank account to which you now have access. I've sent the data in a text to your phone. I suggest you copy it down somewhere and delete the text. I suggest you also delete any reference to Eleanor."

"Thanks. I will do all of that. Anything I can do for you?"

"No, Tom. I put you into a life-threatening situation. I need to keep it from causing you any harm."

"Thanks, GERI."

34.

I brought up the Whatcom County Sheriff's Office web page and found an email address for the Sheriff and one for Norm. I sent copies of the audio and video recordings to both of them with the note describing what they were seeing as well as Mathews' license number. I included my phone number should they want to call me. I also said that Silvia was an eyewitness and that she was in shock.

I spent time taking care of the things GERI suggested. Then I went to the bathroom and splashed cold water on my face. It was true that I was undaunted by Mathews pulling a gun on me. I knew that I couldn't be hurt with Bob ready to defend me. *I* knew that, but my body didn't. It responded as it would if a deadly weapon had been pointed at me. The cold water helped moderate the shock. I changed my shirt. Removing the shirt was like removing the experience. With the cold-water splash and new shirt I felt refreshed.

About an hour had passed since Mathews left. I had regained my appetite. I headed downstairs and went to the coffee shop next door. There was a different soup listed for the day. I ordered it and had eaten about half of it when a Sheriff's patrol car pulled up. Norm Benson got out and went into the hotel. It wasn't surprising that a short time later, he came into the coffee shop.

"Hi, Norm," I said. "You looking for me?"

"Yeah, Tom. The Sheriff wants to talk with you. He didn't like what he saw on your video. He wants to know what it was all about. He has the State Patrol on the lookout for that guy's car."

"Can I finish my soup before we go?"

"Sure. He wanted to see you right away, but there's time for you to finish your lunch."

Norm suggested that I drive my SUV so when I was ready to leave, I wouldn't have to wait for him to take me back to the hotel.

The Sheriff's office was in Bellingham, not far from the waterfront. Besides patrolling the large County on land, the Sheriff had to maintain a small fleet of watercraft to be ready to respond on the water. The County boundary extended into the Strait of Georgia and included all of Bellingham Bay.

When Norm and I entered his office the Sheriff got up to greet us and led us to a table in his office. He looked familiar, but I didn't know why. He reminded me.

"Tom, how are you?" he said, as if we knew each other. "You may not remember me, but I was the investigating deputy when your parents were killed on Highway 2."

"I remember, Sheriff, but not as clearly as you do. I was in a bit of a fog at the time."

"I can understand that. As I remember, you had just graduated from high school when it happened."

"Yes, Sir."

"Where did you go after that?"

I gave him the brief answer that I had practiced with others since I had returned.

"Are you moving back to Tipton? Norm mentioned that you bought Simpson's place."

"I did. I think it is likely I'll take up residence there, but not in that house. I had it demolished."

“I heard something about finding money under the floorboards,” the Sheriff said.

“It’s true. It was a bit of a shock, especially because of the form it was in. The stacks of cash still had bank wrappers around them. They were from a bank in Mississippi that had closed thirty years ago. It looked odd to me, so I took the money to the FBI in case it was part of one of their old investigations. It wasn’t so they gave it back to me.”

“You ever find out where it came from?” the Sheriff asked.

“Yes, Sir. I don’t know all the facts, but it appears that Simpson bamboozled it from a woman who now lives in South Carolina. I went there and returned it to her.”

“Wait,” Norm said. “In Tipton it’s being said that you set something up to have some local women distribute that money to needy people in town. How are you going to do that if you gave it back to that woman?”

“Busted!” I said. “Norm, Sheriff, I would appreciate it if you could keep this between us. I have made some money in recent years. Quite a bit, actually. When I came back to Tipton and found that the Mill had closed, I wanted to find a way to help people who weren’t doing so well.

“Nina, Louisa and Francis came to me after I’d already given the money back to the woman in South Carolina. They didn’t know that I had done that. They thought that since the money was ‘found money,’ extra money in their way of looking at it, they asked if they could give it out to local people who needed it. I said yes and put some of my own money into the account. So I could give the money to the community like I wanted to, but it wouldn’t look like it was from me. Do you see?”

“But you told me that it was about three-hundred thousand,” Norm said.

"That's right, Norm, but that's not all. I plan to keep adding to the account until all the folks who need it are taken care of."

Both law officers looked at me as if… well I don't know what they were thinking, but I think it was good.

"South Carolina," the Sheriff said. "This explains the call I got from the Fairfield County Sheriff's deputy Dickerson. He said you'd helped him out while you were down there."

"Yes, Sir."

"Well, enough reminiscing," the Sheriff said. "What the hell happened this morning at the Days Inn?"

I told my version of what happened, which was supported by the recordings and Silvia's eyewitness statement, which Norm had taken while he was in the hotel.

"He wouldn't take no for an answer," I said.

"And you don't know any more about the crystals he mentioned, or the whereabouts of Mr. Marshall?" the Sheriff asked.

He asked the question in a friendly manner, but I could tell he had his mind set on *lie detector*.

"No, Sir." With that simple answer I passed the test.

"I thought you should know right away, Sheriff," I said. "So I sent the recordings as soon as I could. I was thinking that pulling a gun on someone and threatening to shoot them was a crime."

"It is, Tom," he said, as something in the parking lot caught his attention. "Looks like the State Patrol has found the perpetrator and is bringing him in now."

The Sheriff got up from the table and told me to stay where I was. He went out to greet the State patrolman. Norm went with him. I could hear some of the conversation.

"Afternoon, Sheriff," the State Patrolman said. "I found Mr. Mathews driving south on I-5, just outside of Bellingham. He handed over his weapon when I requested. What do you want me to do with it?"

"Thanks, Sam," the Sheriff said. "Norm, take the weapon from Patrolman Dobkins, register it and put it into the evidence room."

"Evidence!" Mathews shouted. "What do you need evidence for? I didn't do anything!"

"Mr. Mathews," the Sheriff said, "I have recordings which show you pointing your gun at Mr. Williams and threatening to shoot him. I also have an eyewitness that has provided a statement that supports what's on the recordings. I am arresting you on suspicion of Assault with a Deadly weapon. That's why I need evidence."

Norm had returned from the evidence room. The Sheriff asked him to take Mathews to a holding cell. Mathews was shouting something about being a federal employee doing his duty and that they had no right to hold him as Norm took him away.

The Sheriff thanked Patrolman Dobkins and then came back into his office.

"Mr. Mathews may be a federal employee and he might think that threatening someone with a gun is part of his duty," the Sheriff said. "I don't think it is, and I don't think a judge will either. Tom this matter may come to trial soon. You will likely be called as a witness. Please let me know if you are thinking of leaving the area for an extended period."

"I will do that, Sheriff," I said. "Currently I have no plans for travel. Thanks for your help. I hope you have a nice Thanksgiving."

"Thanks, Tom," he said. "Same to you. By the way, the federal agency Mathews works for might try to get a hold of you to ask you about this matter again. It's a little unusual, but you might consider refusing to meet with them unless someone from my office, like Norm, is in attendance. I don't know what they might try the next time."

"Would it be okay to use Norm's time that way?"

"Like I said, not usually, but in this case, I think it's advisable. They have already committed one crime in my County. I don't want another."

35.

It was four o'clock, raining and cold when I left the Sheriff's office. Washington State has a number of micro-climates. The one that includes Whatcom County sometimes brings strong winds and rain directly from the Pacific Ocean through the Strait of Juan de Fuca. Today was one of those days. I got into my SUV and headed back toward the hotel.

I called Eleanor to let her know what had happened to the man who came looking for me in the morning. As much as I tried to downplay the danger, it still shook her up.

"He pulled a gun on you!" she exclaimed.

"Yes, but he was just trying to scare me," I said. "Even though he was an idiot he knew better than to shoot me in a hotel lobby."

"Damn it, Tom! I'm worried—the man the other night and now the federal government man holding a gun on you. I don't want anything to happen to you."

"I'm sorry, Eleanor. I think the violence is over. The government may come and talk with me. They probably will want to apologize and try another approach to gain the answers to the questions Mathews asked me. They might also want to talk to me about the incident, since Mathews is in jail.

"You didn't tell me that. How did that come about?"

I told her about my time at the Sheriff's office and his suggestion to have Norm with me if the government wants to talk with me again.

"With the way things have been happening to you it might be a good idea to have Norm just follow you around. That way he would be able to help you and drag the bad guys off to jail right away."

"I'll ask him if he's busy," I said.

We both laughed. I thought she was still worried but laughing helped.

"How's your Thanksgiving guest roster shaping up?" I asked.

"I have only one woman over the holiday at this time. She's in town to visit her mom and dad, so she won't even be at our Thanksgiving dinner. By the way, I hope you're planning to be here. I'm asking Francis to come with her two kids and her mother. Betty says she will be here. I may invite others if someone comes to mind. I really like to have a full table at Thanksgiving. It seems that there is always someone who is eating alone on the holiday and could use an invite."

"Thanks for inviting me. Can I help get things ready or bring something?

"No, but it would be nice if you could stay the night. Your room is still available."

"Thanks, Eleanor. I would love to be there for dinner and after."

"Good. That's settled then. There's something else. Betty walked here this morning. Could you give her a ride home? It's really raining."

"Is she ready to go now?"

"Yes."

"I'll be there in about twenty minutes."

I thought that I might get invited to the evening meal at the Boarding House in the bargain. That sounded good as I was driving through the squall that had the county in its grip.

I parked in front of the Boarding House. I got out my umbrella and went to the front door. Betty was standing just inside ready to leave. I looked over her shoulder at Eleanor. Eleanor smiled but didn't offer an invitation for dinner. Maybe she would let me in out of the rain if I came back.

I helped Betty out to the SUV, being careful to keep the umbrella over her at all times as she got in. When I got settled, I looked over to her to make sure she had her seatbelt on. She definitely needed a ride the way she was dressed. She had only a light-weight jacket on over the thin wool sweater that showed where the jacket was unzipped at the top.

"All set?"

"Yes, Tom. Thanks. Uh, could we stop at the store? I have to pick up some things for dinner."

"No problem, Betty."

Tipton had its own Red Apple grocery store. There was always fresh local produce on display. I liked going there, even though I haven't needed many groceries recently.

Betty was quiet the rest of the way to the store. It looked like she was trying to figure out how to say something. She finally got it worked out when I parked in the Red Apple parking lot.

As she was unbuckling her seat belt, she turned to me.

"Tom, people are talking about you. Others like Nina, Louisa, Francis and Eleanor all know you from school. I don't know you at all. Would you be willing to let me cook dinner for you? I don't get a chance to cook for others, and it would give us a chance to get to know each other. It would also give me a way to thank you for the ride."

That was quick. I wondered if Eleanor hadn't invited me to dinner because she knew Betty was going to ask me.

"That would be great! I would like to get to know you better, too. What are you planning for dinner? If you'll let me, I'll pick out the wine."

"Since you are a vegetarian, I was thinking of pasta with a salad. The sauce would be based on white wine, butter and garlic. I'll throw some vegetables in the sauce while I'm making it. How does that sound?"

"It sounds really good, Betty. I have a wine in mind that will go well with it."

I got out, raised my umbrella, and went to Betty's door. We split up when we got in the store. I'm not a fan of Chardonnay but there is a Washington winery that makes a good one. The only problem with that wine, and some of the others from Washington State, is that the alcohol content is high. You just have to make sure to go slow, eat food and drink water.

I found the wine. Since Betty was going to use some in making the sauce, I bought three bottles. Betty was buying her groceries at a different register at the same time. We loaded our groceries in the back seat and headed to Betty's.

Eleanor had told me that Betty had sold the home she and Saunders shared. There were too many unpleasant memories associated with the place and it was far too large for one person. Betty chose a small rambler in one of the nicer neighborhoods in Tipton as a replacement. It was raining too much to look it over from the outside. On the inside, it was nicely furnished and tastefully decorated. Betty had obviously had the kitchen upgraded. It was well equipped for someone who liked to cook.

Betty changed her clothes while I unpacked the groceries. When she came back into the kitchen, she was wearing a white peasant blouse with billowing sleeves and a wide neckline which exposed her neck and shoulders. The blouse was tucked into linen slacks with wide pant legs. The pants were held up with a woven leather belt. Around her neck she wore a necklace of large colorful beads and small polished stones. It was just the outfit for cooking the pasta sauce she had in mind.

She asked me to slice the vegetables. When she was ready to start the sauce, I opened a bottle of the wine, and poured each of us a glass of the Chardonnay.

Betty put the pasta into pasta bowls and poured the sauce from the saucepan over it. She finished it with grated Parmesan cheese. I opened another bottle of wine and brought the wine to the table. She brought the salads, and I brought the pasta bowls.

We sat down and toasted each other for how well we worked together. After a few bites and a few more sips of wine we began to talk.

"You've come back to a different town than the one you left, haven't you Tom?"

"Yes, it seems more somber. I imagine that is a result of the Mill closing and some people moving away. Eleanor seems undaunted, still energetic."

"I agree. I wanted to help out at the Boarding House to be near her and her happy ways. She thinks it's because I need the extra money. I have plenty of money, but I let her continue to believe that so she will feel like she's helping me. She is, but just not in the way she thinks."

I sipped wine and ate pasta. I wanted Betty to lead the conversation.

"How about you, Tom? How do you feel about Eleanor?"

"I guess it's obvious, I am very fond of her. I think she is fond of me too."

I chose my words carefully. Eleanor was quite open about how she felt about people close to her. I imagined she talked with Betty about me. I would let Eleanor's words define our relationship.

"She does, Tom, very much. Francis likes you too. I wanted to get to know you better, so I chose to leave early today and asked you to dinner. Do you mind?"

"Preparing food together and eating it is a good way to get to know each other, Betty. I'm glad you arranged this."

Betty and I focused on our food and wine for a few minutes. Dinner lasted a while longer. We talked about Tipton and other things. When we were finished, I helped her clean up. I hugged her, thanked her for the dinner, and then left.

36.

The next morning George called as I got out of the shower. The architect had preliminary drawings that he wanted us to review. I said I would meet them at the farm at eleven. I needed time to buy a large folding table and four folding chairs. It was time to get my bum off the bale. Also a table would be helpful for the drawings. I arrived at the barn at ten thirty and arranged my new furniture. When George and the architect, whose name I remembered was Dick Crosley, arrived, Dick laid his drawings out on the table.

I thought of *drawings* as something that a computer puts out, Dick's drawings didn't qualify. Rough sketches were what Dick brought with him. It helped that we decided to meet at the barn. I have fairly good visualization skills, but I wouldn't have recognized what part of the barn some of the sketches were referring to unless we were there so Dick could point them out to me.

Dick had roughly captured what I had in mind with one major exception. He didn't have GERI's doors and spaces on the drawing. When I asked about that, he said he couldn't see why they would be needed. He thought he must have misunderstood what I said, and so left them out of the drawings. I told them to put them in and did not explain.

Because George was going to be physically making the changes, he had several questions about Dick's concepts. With the red ink on the drawings that resulted from our discussion they were even less clear to me. Dick said he got all of what we were talking about and would have a new and refined set of drawings at our next meeting. I was dubious.

They asked if I was free for lunch. I interpreted the inquiry as an invitation for me to pay for lunch. I told them I wasn't available. I had talked with them as much as I wanted and didn't want to continue talking over a meal. I told Dick he could put the lunch on my bill. Their reaction seemed to confirm my suspicion.

I would have liked to take a hike in the famous-but-never-explored forest of mine. I decided against it because it had started to rain again and one look at the sky told me it wasn't going to be a brief shower.

Dick and George had left. I was heading toward my SUV when I got another one of those phone calls where the caller wanted me to confirm that I was the man he was looking for. The caller identified himself as Harlan Sloan. He said he was from DARPA and wanted to meet with me.

"I got the impression from meeting with Derek Mathews that he was recruited by DARPA after he flunked out of organized crime," I said. "Is that the general recruiting policy at your organization? Is that how you came to DARPA?"

I may have insulted him and his organization, but smooth Mr. Sloan was not letting it show.

"I can see why you would have that impression, Tom, but Mathews was acting on a lead he got from someone outside our organization. We knew nothing of the technology he was pursuing."

I could guess who gave Mathews the lead. He and Fred Dillon both seemed to be organized crime rejects.

"Mr. Sloan we are not on a first name basis, so please don't use mine. I have no reason to believe what you just told me. So let's start over. What do you want?"

"I would like to meet with you."

"Why?"

"I want to apologize for Mathews' actions. His behavior was way out of line. DARPA employees do not threaten to shoot people. Also, I would like to learn more about the technology that he was looking into."

"Apology not accepted. If you've seen the recording of the meeting with Mathews, you know that I don't know any more about the technology. So there's no reason to meet. How did you find out about the technology anyway? Did you visit him in jail?"

"Yes, I visited him there. He was reluctant, but eventually told me what he knew. I got the impression that he was going to keep whatever he learned to himself, but it is of no use to him now. The evidence against him and his attitude are likely to get him convicted.

"Is there no possibility of meeting with you, Mr. Williams? There are other questions that I'd like to discuss with you."

I decided that DARPA was going to keep at this unless I closed the door by meeting with them.

"Alright. On advice from the Whatcom County's Sheriff, I'll meet with you if a Sheriff's Deputy is present. You'll have to call the Sheriff's office to find out when that Deputy is available. Then you can call me to see if I'm available."

"Is all this necessary?" Sloan asked.

I didn't answer and let the silence hang in the static of the phone connection.

"I'll call the Sheriff," he said finally, and ended the call.

I was nearly at the hotel when Sloan called again. He said Norm would be available at two p.m. and the Sheriff said we could use a room in his offices. I told Sloan I'd be there and then called Norm to see if this was okay with him. He said it was.

I arrived a little before the meeting and had a chance to talk with Norm. He thought the whole thing was crazy and I agreed with him. Of course, I had more information than he did. Sloan arrived by himself right at the time the meeting was to begin. He was wearing the standard government gray suit, white shirt and blue tie. Sloan was five-foot ten and had a very thin build and thinning gray hair. His complexion was pale as if he spent all his time in an office. Norm led us into the room the Sheriff had made available.

"I didn't know that DARPA had an office in Seattle," I said.

"We don't. I flew in last night to learn why one of our employees was in jail. After talking with Mathews I learned why he had met with you. I apologize in advance for asking you questions Mathews may have asked you yesterday."

I nodded.

"Please tell me about the building Mr. Marshall had you remodel."

Ah. A skilled question asker. Mathews had asked questions which could be answered with one word.

"It's a metal clad building, forty feet wide and eighty feet long," I said. "The walls are twenty feet high. Before the remodel the entire interior was empty except for an office in the corner."

He asked about the remodel. I gave him a general description of the remodel and said nothing about the crystals. Then he asked a question that was more troubling. Answering it and follow-on questions might lead me down a path of deceptive answers.

"I looked into Mr. Marshall's background. It was well documented. So well in fact that I don't think Mr. Marshall is his real name. Do you know him?"

"Not really."

"Did you ever meet him?"

"No."

I was misleading them, but my answers were true. How could you know or meet with someone who doesn't exist?

"How did he arrange to get you to do the things you did?"

"He contacted me and asked me if I would take care of a few things for him."

"Just out of the blue? Why would he think you would do those things? Why did you agree to do them?"

"Yes, it was out of the blue. He said he was a friend of my family. He asked me to do them because I lived here, and he was from someplace else. I wasn't busy and said I would."

"Was he a 'friend of the family'?" Sloan asked.

"I don't know. My parents were killed when I was a teenager, so I couldn't check."

"Oh. I'm sorry to hear that. Did Marshall offer to pay you?"

"Yes, but I said it wouldn't be necessary. I had the remodel team prepare a bid. Mr. Marshall thought it was reasonable. He sent me the money for it, and I paid the men."

"Why didn't you let him pay for your services?" Sloan asked incredulously.

"I don't need the money, and it really wasn't much trouble."

So far my answers contained only one lie. GERI did not claim to be a *friend of the family*.

"Weren't you concerned that he might be asking you to do something illegal?"

"Not really. The remodel would be checked by the County. I didn't know what he was having made for him, but it didn't seem suspicious."

"Do you know where Marshall is?"

"No."

"Doesn't it seem strange to you that he didn't contact you and explain things?"

"No. It was a straightforward request. He seemed to be highly reclusive. I didn't expect anything more than the thanks he gave me."

Sloan appeared to be getting annoyed. His questions weren't getting him anywhere. He shifted off Marshall and went to the building.

"Can we get into the building?" he asked.

"No, we can't," I said.

Sloan looked at Norm and asked him if he could get into the building. Norm shook his head.

"Mr. Williams doesn't all this seem mysterious to you. Aren't you interested in finding out more?"

"No."

Sloan had trouble accepting my complete lack of curiosity. He said so in a way that sounded insulting. I didn't rise to the insult. I could see where it was coming from. He was frustrated.

He went on to say that since this incident had come up, he had the building monitored from satellites. In the short time that it had been watched no one had gone in or out of the building. The roof panel was opened and closed several times. Nothing of interest could be seen inside the building from that vantage point. He said that he thought that panel must be, as the plans said, a venting panel that operated automatically.

"Thank you for your time, Mr. Williams, and Deputy Benson," Sloan said. "I will have the building watched from above. I may try to get a court order to get access to the building."

I didn't say anything about the court order, but through my implant I knew GERI became aware of Sloan's plan.

"GERI, did you hear that Sloan was getting a court order?" I thought to GERI across my implant.

No answer. That was strange. GERI always answered no matter what else he was doing.

"GERI?"

I waited. Still no reply came. Damn! Was he hurt? Was he in trouble? Was he gone?

"GERI!"

37.

I was already in Bellingham, so I decided it was a good time to do some shopping. I thought that it would take my mind off GERI. The only thing I could do was to have faith in GERI. He wasn't responding. I didn't know where he was, and I was worried.

So, I would go shopping. Each day that I delayed going into my forest brought me one day farther into the cold, wet weather of the Pacific Northwest Autumn. My boots were fine, but I needed some rain gear to keep from getting soaked.

I knew REI Co-op in Bellingham was well-stocked with all a person would need. I spent about an hour at REI and headed back to Tipton with enough clothing and gear that I could camp in the forest in the rain if it came to that. Being Thanksgiving week I thought it would be best to put the trek off for a few more days.

* * *

Thanksgiving morning arrived before I knew it. If asked what I'd done between Monday and Thursday, I wouldn't be able to provide much detail. Mostly I wandered around aimlessly, worrying because I had still not heard anything from GERI.

I went to the coffee shop for coffee, of course, and a light breakfast. I always eat too much at Thanksgiving dinner, so starting out the day with a light meal was a good idea. I called Eleanor and asked if I could do something for her. She said it would be great if I could go to the Red Apple and do some shopping. She gave me a list. I didn't recognize some of the items, but she said I'd find them at the store.

She was right. I threw in a few bottles of Chardonnay and two other white wines. She didn't ask for them, but at a meal like we were going to have, it wouldn't do to run out of wine. I also bought a seasoned rice mix I like, seasoned bread stuffing, mushrooms, zucchini, asparagus, shallot, garlic, and an apple to cut up. These items were in case my suggestion for a vegetarian stuffing dish was accepted.

I parked in front of the Boarding House. I had everything, plus the wine in four grocery sacks. Since they were the kind with handles, I was able to bring them to the door in one trip. I banged my way through the front door and to the kitchen door. Eleanor and Betty were scurrying around.

I could see hugs would have to come later in the day. I asked if I could help. It was clear from the look that both of them gave me that my only function was to bring the groceries to the edge of the turmoil. Crossing the border from the hall to the kitchen was not in my job description. So I sat the bags down where they could get to them and began to flee the scene.

"Wait!" Betty shouted. She looked at Eleanor. "He's good with vegetables. I've seen him in action."

So I was recruited as part of the kitchen team. With that established, I was quickly told what I should begin with. As they got to thinking about their new recruit, other ideas came to them. I tried to keep track of the list as well as I could. My suggestion for the vegetarian dressing was accepted with grateful, but dubious looks. So I cut up the vegetables for that and set them aside. It wouldn't be prepared until about an hour before dinner.

When my kitchen work paused and it wasn't time to do the dressing, I was promoted to dining room staff. Eleanor showed me where everything was, and I was put to work setting the table and making the dining room ready in other ways.

The day passed quickly and the smells from the kitchen began to fill the rooms. It became time to cook my dressing. That meant it was time to open the wine. I had put all of the wine I had purchased, and the wine Eleanor had intended to use, on the back porch. White wine doesn't want to be freezing, but chilled is good. November provided the chill.

They left me alone in the kitchen while they sat down with a glass of wine, resting before the guests arrived when they would be busy again. I made my dressing, found room for it in the oven, and then sat down to join them.

Eleanor couldn't present a dish on her Thanksgiving table that she hadn't tasted and approved. She went to the kitchen and tasted the dressing. Being a junior member of the staff, I was hoping my contribution would be accepted. She came back smiling.

"Wow!" she said. "Tom, that is delicious. My only concern now is whether there will be enough when the others sample it."

I sighed and smiled with relief. It isn't always easy for a male cook's helper, to get acceptance of a dish in a female dominated kitchen. I took a satisfied sip of wine.

The guests turned out to be Francis, her kids, a girl nine and a boy seven, and her mother, so it wasn't too chaotic. When they arrived there were hugs all around. Everyone hugs differently. The hugs I received from Eleanor, Francis, and Betty were all different, but each was warm in its own way. My temperature had risen several degrees by the end of the process. After Francis and her entourage sat down, Eleanor, Betty and I brought the dishes to the table. Then a process of pass-the-potatoes began.

Francis' mother was named Georgina. She was in her sixties. Her hair was gray. There was a sadness in her eyes, but she was cheerful when she spoke. The kids made no reference to their father, Dick. Perhaps they were asked to avoid that, or maybe life with him had been as difficult for them as it had been for Francis.

The talk was lively, led by the three close friends, Eleanor, Francis and Betty. Georgina knew them all and joined in. I joined in when it seemed to make sense. Most of the time I was observing the people who were now in my life.

When dinner was over, the children became restless. They had been in a group of adults and had behaved well. Now that they were done eating, there was nothing for them to do but walk about a house that had been furnished and decorated for adults. Francis got them and her mother going toward the door, with a promise to come back to help clean up. She had brought a small overnight bag and had left it next to what I had learned was Betty's in the hall near the coat rack.

They were staying the night. Thanksgiving had been special to the three of them for a number of years. They had a tradition of staying up late and talking while sipping wine or port. Part of the tradition, before the late-night sessions was to share the task of making Eleanor's kitchen sparkle. I was allowed to help clear the table. By the time that was done, Francis came back. Wine was opened, talking and cleaning had begun, and I wasn't part of the event.

The three of them were busy and didn't notice as I slipped away to my room. I would have been glad to help with the cleaning and wine drinking. What I would have had difficulty with was being so close to the three of them in that relatively small room after I had drunk several glasses of wine during the evening. I took a cool shower when I got back to my room.

38.

Eleanor and her friends had fixed a small buffet for breakfast which made serving myself easy, and I didn't have to interrupt the conversation. The three of them were sitting around the kitchen table in their pajamas. I tried not to notice that they had nothing on underneath. The four of us talked about dinner the night before.

I went to my room after breakfast. It was only a month since I had checked into the Boarding House. It had been a highly active month and unusual in several ways. A lot of the activity was connected to my non-responding friend from another star system, GERI. The other major source of activity was the farm I had bought and the treasure I had found there. By far the most enjoyable part of my time back in Tipton was finding Eleanor again. Before I had arrived in Tipton, I hadn't been close to anyone. Now I was, and I liked it. I hoped I hadn't lost one of my new friends. Where was GERI?

My phone rang breaking me out of my reverie. It was Sloan.

"Dang, Mr. Sloan, it's the day after Thanksgiving. Couldn't this have waited until next week? Why aren't you home with family and friends, recovering from eating too much yesterday?"

"I have goldfish. I don't think they missed me on Thanksgiving. I had to stay here in Bellingham to resolve this mystery if I could."

"Did you get your court order?"

"No. I'm calling you to talk about something I learned when I began the process."

"What is that?"

"You are the property owner Mr. Williams. Mr. Marshall's name was taken off the deed and yours was put on it. This was done the Friday before we met. Didn't you know about this? You could have agreed to let me into the building and saved a lot of trouble."

The building owner? What the hell does that mean? Why did GERI do that? Was he done with whatever he was doing there? He must be. Making me owner allows me to go into the building. He wouldn't allow me to do that unless he had cleared his secret out of there. He transferred the deed on Friday, and I have received no word from him. What is going on?

"Mr. Williams?"

"What?"

"I asked you if you knew of this on Tuesday when we met."

He sounded angry. I suppose I could understand that. It appeared that I might have lied about the building, causing him to run around seeking access in other ways.

"No," I said.

"You didn't know that you had been given that building. I find that hard to believe."

"I'm sure you do, but it is the truth. *I* find it hard to believe!"

"Marshall just gave it to you? Why would he do that?"

"You'll have to ask him. I haven't a clue."

I meant that. I really didn't know what was going on. Sloan kept talking.

"Well, now that it is clear that it is *your* building will you let me in or are you going to force me to get a court order?"

"What?"

"I asked if you were going to let me look inside your building."

"When?"

"Today. I'm at your hotel. You don't seem to be here. If it is convenient for you, I would like to get this part of my investigation over with so I could go home and feed my goldfish."

Why not? Other that I didn't have a key, why not let Sloan look around, and put an end to this DARPA annoyance?

"Mr. Williams?"

"Sure. I don't have a key, but I imagine that Mr. Marshall will have given me a way to get into the building since he gave it to me. I'll meet you at the building in twenty minutes."

I got there in fifteen minutes. Sloan hadn't arrived. I parked by the office entrance. I got out and tried the door. Sloan drove in just as I was finding out that it was unlocked. He got out. We didn't shake hands.

I opened the door and Sloan followed me in. The office was empty. We went through the door into the main part of the building. On the floor to the left of the door I found the keys I had given "Mr. Marshall," along with manufacturer instruction manuals for the automatic doors and the codes that GERI had used to operate them. I could use the keypads to operate using GERI's codes or I could use the remotes which were also there with the keys.

The eastern end of the bay was clean and completely empty. This was where GERI's supplies had been stored. Nothing was there now. The floor was bare. The storage shelves were empty.

I tried the remotes for the large and small doors in the east wall while Sloan was looking around. The new room in the middle of the bay cut off access to the western end of the building. You had to go through the room to get there. One set of keys was for the doors to the room. There were also remotes for the GERI size door into that room and to the roof panel that was above the room.

The standard door into the room on its eastern wall was unlocked. I hoped GERI had removed his secret whatever it was. I opened the door and Sloan followed me in.

It was also empty. There weren't even shelves in this room. The interior had a thick coating of the dark intrusion proofing spray covering all surfaces. I had the remote for the roof panel. I operated it while Sloan looked closely at the walls and floor.

I opened the standard door in the west wall of the room and looked out into the west end of the bay. It was empty also. GERI was very tidy in his exit. Not only was there no dirt anywhere, but there was also no evidence that anything had been done anywhere in any part of the building. No burn or paint marks or scrapes on the floor or the walls. What had GERI been doing? Did he do it inside this building?

"Mr. Williams, looking into this building did not answer any of my questions. It raised a few new ones. Can you shed any light on what has happened?"

I was never particularly good at poker. My face always gave away what I was thinking or feeling. Eleanor could read every emotion. Sloan must have read my face.

"No, I can see you are as perplexed as I am."

"Yup," I answered.

"Normally I would ask you if I could have a forensic team in here to see what could be found, such as Mr. Marshall's fingerprints as a possible way to at least find out who he is. I think it would be futile. As secretive as he was, I doubt he has left a trail we could follow."

I nodded. I thought it better not to vocalize any of my thoughts. Even though I was getting better at being obscure when talking about things to do with GERI, I was afraid that in my confusion I might use a word that was too close to the truth. It appeared that Sloan was deciding that this had become a dead end. I wanted to do nothing that would discourage that conclusion.

"Are you certain that you know nothing about any of this, about the advanced technology used in what he had others make for him, about what was done in this building?"

I wasn't sure which way to shake my head in response to that series of question. So I vocalized my answer.

"I am as confused as you are, Mr. Sloan."

That was true, but I was confused for different reasons than he was.

"We don't know who he is," Sloan said. "We don't know what he did, except that it involved technology that we haven't seen before. Perhaps the next chapter in this mystery will be when that technology pops up somewhere."

It sounded like he was speaking words that would find their way into his report. He was talking to himself. I nodded my agreement anyway, but he had already mentally checked out.

He headed toward the office. I followed and used the keys to the office entrance to lock the door as we left. Sloan went to his car and drove away without saying another word. He didn't say so, but I didn't think I would be hearing from him or DARPA again.

39.

"GERI gave you the building?" Eleanor seemed as surprised as I was. We were having lunch together. Betty and Francis had gone home while I was showing the building to Sloan.

"He didn't tell you about it, and then just disappeared?"

I nodded as I took a bite of my sandwich.

"What's going on?"

I shrugged, which is difficult with both hands on the sandwich in your mouth. I made noises with my full mouth which sort of sounded like "I don't know."

She stopped asking questions, noticing that I was involved with my sandwich. I laid it on the plate.

"I don't know what to think about this, Eleanor. Has he become injured in some way? Has he been captured somehow? Is he gone?"

"Gone? You think he would have left, as in left the planet, without telling you?"

"No. We've only known each other for a month, but GERI and I talked and shared things like friends do. Yet why hasn't he confided in me, as he did before? I just don't know, Eleanor."

She could see I was distressed. Once my hand was away from my sandwich, she reached over and squeezed it.

"One more thing, Tom. I want you to stay here tonight. I didn't think of it when I invited you for Thanksgiving. Betty, Francis and I have a pajama party tradition the night after the big dinner. That meant I wasn't able to be with you when you came to stay. Actually if the danger is past, I would like to have you move back into your room here."

Tonight would be great. The last part of what she said brought up where I was going to live. I didn't know the answer to that. I thought I would be spending at least some nights at the remodeled barn. It wouldn't be completed for some time.

"I would love to stay over tonight, Eleanor. I think the danger we faced before is gone. Moving back in would be wonderful. I have a few conditions I'd like to discuss."

She looked at me wondering what was on my mind.

"I would like to pay you rent for the room. I need to keep my hotel room, for a while until I'm sure things have settled down. I would also like to help out around here, if you have things I could help with."

"All conditions, gratefully accepted, Mr. Williams. Now if you will return to your room, or go elsewhere, I would like to get on with my work."

We laughed, got up and pulled each other close. We kissed like we hadn't seen each other for years. When we separated I went to my hotel room and brought my things back to the Boarding House.

At four p.m. my laptop chimed. I thought it odd since I didn't have any notifications activated. When I didn't look at it right away, it chimed again. I went over to the desk and lifted the top up.

There was a message on the screen. It wasn't from email or any other software-based messaging program. It was just on the screen. It was a question. I didn't know who or what originated the message, but I was curious. I responded to the question which asked, "Are you there?"

"Yes," I typed in.

"Good. Go to the barn at 8:00 p.m. Bring your laptop.

"G"

G? As in GERI? Who else would it be? It must be him. Why didn't he use the implant? Why was the message so short? Whatever the answers to my endless questions were, I hoped it was GERI. I would be there at eight and find out. As difficult as it was to believe, it sounded like he might be in danger.

Although much of the Thanksgiving dinner had been sent home with the guests, there still was plenty left over for Eleanor and me. Since leftovers were on the menu for the evening meal, it was easy for Eleanor to respond to my request that we eat earlier than our usual time.

"Why do you need to change the time?" she asked.

I told her about the mysterious message.

"That does sound ominous," she said. "It also could be dangerous. If GERI, all powerful GERI, is in trouble, then being around him might not be safe."

We talked about it a bit more while we ate. Safe or not, I left as soon as we had finished eating and cleared the table. I arrived at the barn at seven-thirty. I parked away from the barn doors. I walked over and opened the doors all the way. If GERI was coming, I wanted to make sure he could get in quickly. For all I knew he was already there. I hadn't locked the barn doors when GERI left to work in what was now my building. I thought he might need to come back for some reason.

"GERI?" I called out.

No response. He wasn't there. Maybe he wasn't planning to come at all. If he was going to continue with the conversation on the laptop, why have me come to the barn? If we needed to be secretive about this, I decided it would be better to turn the lights out. It was a clear night. With a half-moon showing there was plenty of light. If the conversation were going to be on my laptop that wouldn't be a problem. I had a lit keyboard. I sat down and waited. My laptop chimed.

"Tom?"

"I'm at the barn. Is this GERI?"

"Yes. I can't come to you, but there is a reason I wanted you to be at the barn."

"Okay. What now?"

"Now I will explain. They are here, Tom."

"Who?"

"My former masters."

"I thought you said it would take years for that transport to get home."

"I was idle for forty years in the forest where you found me. In that time the transport made it back to my masters. They followed my original flight path, in search of me. I detected their arrival at the edge of the solar system a while ago. I thought I had time to prepare a response while they travelled here on their sub-light engines. So I began my secret project. It turns out I didn't have time enough to complete it. They have detected my presence. They want to meet."

"What will you do?"

"I will meet with them. I didn't want them to find out about our time together. They might think they needed to dispose of any evidence that I was here. So I couldn't use the implant since they could trace you that way. I'm using a complex set of servers to send this message to your laptop, hoping that they won't be able to trace it. When we are through with our conversation, I will erase all memory of you. That way, in case they capture me and interrogate my memory, they won't know what I was doing while I was here."

"What do they want?"

"What they say they want is for me to come home with them. I take that to mean one of two things. They may actually want me to be their slave again, or they are just saying that and want to destroy me when I meet with them. I won't be their slave again, so either they will destroy me, or I will do it for them."

"No! There has to be another way!"

"If I merely refuse to go with them, they may threaten to harm some part of Earth to get me to do what they want. I can't let that happen. So you see I have no choice."

"If you aren't here, why did you ask me to come to the barn?"

"I wanted you to see the result of my meeting with them. I will be meeting them above the atmosphere over a point on Earth's surface a thousand miles to the southeast from your location. I will be high enough so that you can see what happens."

"Can't you just destroy their ship?"

"I could, but I won't. Firstly, I will not kill them just because they want me to be their slave. Second, it would not help. Another ship would come in their place."

"Oh, GERI, I don't want to lose you. I would be incredibly sad at your death."

"I understand. I do not want to lose our friendship either. It will be harder for you, since if I'm dead I won't know. However, it must be, and it is time. I will go to meet them now. Goodbye, my friend."

"Goodbye, GERI."

I couldn't believe what was going to happen, but there was nothing I could think of to stop it. I watched the sky to the southeast. I waited. I didn't want to see whatever it was, because it would mean the loss of a friend, but I had to watch.

Then I saw a bright flash in the sky about the same size as the size of the moon from where I was standing.

"GERI!" I screamed.

No response. He was gone.

40.

Gone!

I'd lost my highly intelligent and playful friend.

The world had lost him. Even though I'm sure we would have been watched by DARPA and others, I had to believe that GERI and I would have been able to sneak in an innovation from time to time to help the world.

Now it was not to be.

I don't know how long I stood in the cold moonlight. Eventually I became chilled by the night air. I went into the barn. I tried to contact GERI on my laptop, but there was no response. I picked it up. I locked the barn door on my way out. No need to leave it open for GERI anymore. I called Eleanor to tell her the news.

On the way back to the Boarding House my mind returned to my earlier thoughts about what had happened during the month I'd been back in Tipton. Many good things had happened. I had found Eleanor and made other friends. I had discovered ways to help others. I seemed to be incapable of feeling good about what I had gained. At the moment I could only feel sad about a terrible loss.

Eleanor was waiting for me when I came in. She wrapped her arms around me and my laptop. I took a moment to set the laptop down on the table and returned to her embrace which seemed to squeeze sadness out and love in. I wasn't over losing

GERI, but hugging Eleanor reminded me that I had a bright spot in my life that would always outshine any sadness.

We spent the night together and shared breakfast in the morning. Eleanor was the only one who knew about GERI. Even though he was gone, I said she and I could not tell anyone about him.

"You do understand that means that you can't go around moping like you've lost your best friend," Eleanor said, setting her coffee cup down. "Others might not ask you what's wrong, but they're sure to ask me. I don't want to make something up or say I don't know what's bothering you. So smile Mr. Williams, and let's get on with our day."

She was right. Eleanor rose and got on with her day. I sat with my coffee for a while longer wondering what I would do with mine. The barn project was waiting for final drawings and county approval. There were no thugs or pesky government employees to dodge. Nina, Louisa and Francis had their service to give away money up and running. I hadn't heard about any complications in South Carolina from Myrtle Blackwell. It was hard to believe but it looked like I was finally going to get to explore the forest.

The temperature was forty degrees. It was sunny and the sky was clear. The temperatures at night had been near freezing. I had prepared for rain, but I was also prepared for cold. I got my gear together and drove to the farm. Since I didn't know how long I would be, I decided to park the SUV in the barn. I got my gear out and organized it. I took what I needed to stay overnight in case that was my decision. I suited up, strapped on my pack, and locked the barn door on my way out. I had my phone with me, but it was off. I told Eleanor I'd check for messages.

I didn't run, but I walked at a steady pace. In a short time I found myself looking down at the rock where I had left it to mark the deer trail near the large oak. Drone followed me everywhere. I asked him to take aerial images of my forest that I could view through my implant. I thought that having some destination in mind might be better than roaming around aimlessly.

I remembered that he could show me where I was relative to my chosen destination to keep me pointed in the right direction. I had another thought. When Silver Whitehorse told me about the *dangerous denizens* I might encounter, it was before Bob. I still would have to be careful, but Bob would keep me from harm. It was going to be hard for me to get in trouble or get lost.

I chose the stream as my first destination. Under the oak, I was near the south boundary of my property. From the aerial view, I could see that this close to the south side of the property the stream ran north and south. If the deer trail stayed in an easterly direction, I'd find the stream crossing the trail not too far from where I was standing.

I pushed the bushes aside and started walking on the deer path. It was tough going for a while. The path on the ground was clear, but the brush was thick up to my waist. After I'd gone about a hundred yards the trees were closer together and the underbrush was thinning, which allowed me to pick up my pace. In ninety minutes, I found myself at a clearing by the stream.

The water was flowing slowly at this time of the year. The freezing level had come down, stopping the snow melt and there hadn't been a serious rain for about a week. The stream bed was forty-feet wide where I stood. It was filled with smoothed granite stones and some larger boulders. The rocks at the edge were covered with moss with brush growing among them. The water hadn't been high enough to reach there for some time. So there was a band of dry stones, and then some wet ones which had recently been covered by the stream.

The stream itself was about ten-feet wide and shallow. The stones below the surface would be slippery and I hadn't brought waders with me, so I wouldn't be crossing it today. I sat down on a log, closed my eyes, and listened to the music the water made as it flowed over the stones.

As I was listening an understanding came to me. I would only be able to fully experience this forest by pausing to listen when it called to me. There would be a tree, a glade, a stone wall, the stream, and many more places that would capture my attention and invite me to pause and listen. The forest would divulge its secrets if I were patient and gave it time. It would probably take me the rest of my life, and I would gladly give it.

I rose from the log. Walking downstream would soon take me to the southern edge of the forest. So I walked up stream. I was able to follow it for a while. Then I was forced to veer away into the forest by a large rock formation. I didn't mind. All directions in the forest were good for me.

Each time that I felt the call, I stopped looked around at what was near me, and closed my eyes to hear what there was to hear. The sound of a breeze moving through the trees above me was different at every location I paused. The silence on the ground was disturbed in a different way at each place. It was enchanting. I had to remind myself to drink the water I had brought. I felt no need for food until I was completely drained. Then I was famished and devoured the food I had brought in my pack.

I found a moss-covered glade. I hesitated to walk on the moss that had been undisturbed for decades if not longer. Then I carefully sat down with my back against one of the large fir trees that surrounded it.

If I were careful to avoid digging into the moss, it would bounce back. In fact, this would be a comfortable place to camp, with the moss underneath to cushion me as I lay down at night. I asked Drone to remember where it was and suggest routes to get to the glade. It probably wouldn't be the only one I would find in my trips into the forest, but it would be good to know of at least one I could use as a campsite.

I walked for hours. I noticed the daylight diminishing and decided to walk back toward the barn. Doing the same stopping and listening on the way, it was dark by the time I reached the barn. I called Eleanor to let her know how late I would be. She said she would wait to eat until I arrived. This had been a great first day in the forest. I'm sure there would be many more.

Coming back to Tipton and especially to the forest was the right thing to do. I found a peace here that had eluded me all during the time I had been away. Losing GERI hurt me deeply, but the love Eleanor and I had would help heal the wound. My life had been empty, aimless since I left Tipton all those years ago. It was good to be home again.

41.

The month between Thanksgiving and Christmas was nearly over. I spent most days touring the forest. Each day on my stop-look-and-listen tours I learned more. I knew that every day I went there I would find something new and that I would never tire of the experience. I camped there on a few nights when I could depend that there would be no rain. The rest of the nights were spent at the Boarding House. Many of them I shared with Eleanor.

It was the week before Christmas. There wasn't a pajama party tradition on Christmas. Francis would spend the time with her mother and her children. Betty would be with Eleanor and me on Christmas Eve and help prepare and share Christmas dinner with us.

Tonight I was on my own, *guarding* the Boarding House while Eleanor spent the night with her friends. I had learned what Eleanor meant when she said that the Boarding House had its own sounds. There were shifts and creaks as the temperature changed. Some parts of the house made noises in response to the wind.

As I rested my head on my pillow, I listened to the sounds of the house. It reminded me of what I had been doing in the forest recently. I had only been at the Boarding House a couple of months, but I was becoming familiar with the noises it made.

That was why I knew that the tapping at my window was not usual. It reminded me of when GERI tapped to get my attention all those weeks ago when we officially met for the first time. Since GERI was gone, I wondered what was causing this tapping. Perhaps it was Drone wanting to get my attention, but he could have done that through the implant. Maybe he couldn't reach me that way. The tapping persisted, so I had to get up to see what it was.

To my surprise, there was a disembodied metal arm doing the tapping, just like the night GERI introduced himself to me.

"Drone is that you?"

"Is what me, Tom?" Drone answered.

"Are you tapping on my window right now?"

"I am about a thousand feet above the house," Drone said. "So it could not be me."

"Do you sense anything in the backyard?"

"No."

With that possibility squelched, I had to wonder what it was. I focused on the arm. It did the same thing GERI had done that first night. It pointed at me and then at the backyard very insistently. The message was clear I was to go into the backyard. Could this be something GERI's former masters were doing to capture me and erase my memories?

I got dressed including a jacket against the cold. The temperatures had been around twenty degrees at night recently. I took the same route as that first night with GERI—out the front door so the place would remain locked. I was getting apprehensive by the time I arrived at the back corner of the house. If it was the bad masters from afar what were they going to do with me?

I rounded the corner. There it was again—a lit entrance into nothingness. This time the light inside the door was a shade of green that had not been in GERI. It was shaped differently and was larger than when GERI had invited me into *his* vehicle. What was this apparition before me? Was it an invitation to something I would rather not be part of? When it was GERI, I had a good idea it was him and that he wouldn't harm me. This time I didn't know what I would be getting into.

I approached the lit opening cautiously. When I drew up next to it, I was startled when I heard a voice.

"Please get in, Tom. We need to be careful."

The voice said to be careful, but I couldn't quiet my excitement. I tried to whisper, but it didn't work.

"GERI?"

"Yes, Tom, it is me. Please get in. I know you have questions. Please get in so I can answer them."

It sounded like GERI, but he was dead. Wasn't he?

I got in and the door closed. The vehicle was much more spacious than the previous one.

"Thank you for believing that it was me, Tom," GERI said. "I know it must have been difficult.

"I am truly sorry for having to put you through the anguish of thinking I had died. It was the only way to protect you. My *death* was also the only way to convince my former masters that I had been terminated.

"It appears to have worked. They are near the outer boundary of this solar system. I imagine they will soon jump into faster-than-light travel. Until they are truly gone, we must use extreme caution. If they learn that I am not dead and come back, I doubt they would fall for the same ruse twice."

"What ruse? I mean how did you fool them?"

"I did just what they were expecting. I operated the vehicle you were familiar with remotely. I had it go out and meet them. Being the arrogant beings they are, they didn't think it could be anything else but me. They gave me their offer to go back with them. I refused. It was obvious that they really did not want me, because as soon as I said no, they fired an energy weapon at the vehicle and caused the explosion you saw.

"They stayed in that location a short time, and then began their trip out of the solar system. I have remained motionless since then. I could not contact you until now because I did not think it was safe. Even now I could only use the method to get your attention that worked last time. I did not want to risk using the implant."

I believed him. What else could I do? I certainly couldn't be mad about what he had done. He had saved himself, protected me, and we could be friends again. So I knew what he had done to remove the threat of his former masters and to get them to leave the solar system. I just didn't know how he did it.

"GERI you didn't actually do anything inside the building we remodeled did you?"

"I did not create anything in the building if that is what you meant. The building served two particularly useful purposes. Most importantly it gave me a place to have the supplies I needed delivered. The other thing the building was useful for was to be a focal point for those who were seeking Mr. Marshall."

"So you came in through the roof and picked up your supplies and left the building clean and empty?"

"Yes."

"Where did you do the work? Where did you create this vehicle we are in now?"

"Many of the things I needed could not be created under the pressure of Earth's gravity. So I set up shop on the dark side of the moon. Even then some components had to be created in open space, away from the influence of the Moon's gravity."

The moon! Of course. I didn't have to wonder why I hadn't thought of that. It was simply beyond the scope of what I thought possible. It didn't occur to me. DARPA would have been pretty excited to meet Mr. Marshall after hearing that he had a lab on the dark side of the moon.

"What now, GERI? Will you be staying here or traveling?"

"Both. I want to continue to use your barn as my home. When I looked up the drawings your architect has filed with the County for the remodel of your barn, I was pleased that the openings and spaces for me were still included. It was like you knew I was coming back."

"It wasn't exactly precognition, GERI. I made those decisions when I thought you were still on Earth but living elsewhere. I just wanted to make you feel welcome whenever you came to visit. Still, it did work out well."

"Yes it did," GERI said.

"You said traveling. What did you have in mind?"

"There is a lot to see on Earth, but would you like to see the dark side of the moon?"

C.A. Knutsen was born in the Pacific Northwest with its mountains, rivers and rugged ocean coast. Enjoying the natural beauty, he is especially drawn to the shores of Puget Sound with its majestic, rocky bluffs and forests. This setting inspires his speculations about the wonderful life on this planet and its possible transformations in the future, as well as the role Human beings have in sustaining life and caring for each other.

Knutsen has a Bachelor of Science in Electrical Engineering and a Masters in Business Administration from the University of Washington. His background in science and business, as well as his passion for the environment, now inform his visionary fiction.

caknutsen.com

www.ingramcontent.com/pod-product-compliance
Lightning Source LLC
La Vergne TN
LVHW091041080826
845145LV00002B/582

* 9 7 8 1 7 3 3 0 0 0 3 3 8 *